Tucker's Perfect Day

A Tucker McBride Novel

Doris Gaines Rapp, Ph. D.

Tucker's Perfect Day
A Tucker McBride Novel

Doris Gaines Rapp

Daniel's House Publishing

Huntington, Indiana

Copyright 2021 Doris Gaines Rapp
Huntington, Indiana 46750

website: www.dorisgainesrapp.com
contact: dorisgainesrapp@gmail.com
blog: www.tuckermcbrideintheclassroom.com

This book is a work of historic/biographic fiction. Some characters, incidents, and conversations are products of the author's imagination and used here fictitiously. The timeline of the actual events, is compressed in some instances, and expanded in others.

Cover design is a drawing by the author, Doris Gaines Rapp, and stock imagery from @Dreamstime.com, put in place by @Debi Lindhorst/The Type Galley. Other images are from the internet.

Bible Verses - taken from the King James Version (KJV)

Library of Congress Control Number: 2021913931

ISBN-13: 978-1-7365110-4-6 (paperback)
ISBN-13: 978-1-7365110-2-2 (eBook)

Warning
Tucker McBride rarely thinks before he acts. Learn from Tucker. Do not try Tucker's stunts.

Glossary
For an unfamiliar word with an asterisk (*) beside it, go to the back of the book for a definition or picture.

5

Dedication

Tucker McBride's Perfect Day, a novel dedicated to all those who look for a perfect day and never find it.
There is nothing perfect in life. Life is about loving others and making room for everyone. Only perfect love is perfect.

Acknowledgements

A big thank you to the writers' group, Soli deo Gloria (to God be the Glory). Your presence and positive encouragement are blessings. Thanks for sharing your faith in God.

Thank you, Vicki Borgman, for your willingness to read, *Tucker's Perfect Day.* The fact that Tucker McBride is actually your father is just another plus.

Thanks to two new pre-pub readers, Donna Nehring and Ann Peacock. Thanks for your interest in *Tucker* and your helpful suggestions. All on my readers are a blessing. Those who take the time to sift through each detail, editing Tucker's antics, are a tremendous help.

Thank you, Debi Lindhorst of The Type Galley in Warren, Indiana. I have few computer skills. Thank goodness you're gifted in geek.

I also thank others who willing read pre-publication copies of *Tucker's Perfect Day.* You find what I never even see, yet know it is there.

Table of Contents

Chapter One
Northern Indiana Thursday, October 30, 1947

The big square house on the corner in Dunlap, Indiana was full of love and full of people. From the basement to the attic, every crook and cranny had a piece of their lives tucked inside. Tim, Tucker's brother, was away in the Marine Corps. But Tucker, and his two sisters, Betsy, and Carolyn still lived with Grandpop and Gramma Moyer. Uncle Jacob, a single man with an appetite for reading everything he could find, was their legal guardian. Jacob had the front, east bedroom. Gramma's cousin, Sarah, moved in and took over Tim's room, after her husband, Steven, died. It seemed each morning had to clear space for the new day.

Tucker sat straight up in bed. His shepherd dog, Joe, whined with a strange new whistling sound. The boy shook his head. *What time is it?* He picked up the key-wind alarm clock on the nightstand and yawned. It was 6:30 AM.

Tucker wanted to stay in bed. Since it was Thursday, a school day, that thought was impractical. Each day, the entire eighth-grade faculty of Concord Middle School staged their defense and braced for the arrival of Tucker McBride. He had to be prepared to mount the offense. In the stillness of the early morning, Joe's whine cut through the air and hung there. *Why are you barking, Boy?*

Tucker stretched to the sound of a distant robin. Laying back down, he thought of Gramma's recitation. *The north wind doth blow, and we shall have snow. What will poor robin do then, poor thing?* [1]

"Joe, it won't be long until snow could cover everything. It is Indiana, ya know." The dog didn't seem to care. Tucker cringed, first, at the thought of snow, and second, at the image of the other guys teasing him when they heard him recite childhood poetry. Stretching out, he threw off the covers, enjoying the sound of nature filtering through the morning blur. He'd have to attend to Joe's needs, but caring for a decorated War Dog was no problem. It was a privilege.

Uncle Jacob had responded to the War Department's call for good, trainable dogs. World War II needed so many soldiers they asked for dogs to help patrol and carry messages. Jacob volunteered the family dog, Joe, for the K-9 Corps. Joe delivered messages along the treacherous front lines to the commanders in the front. He also walked guard duty with those who protected the perimeter of the camps in the fighting area. Injured several times, Joe earned his own Purple Heart, the Medal of Honor, and another medal Tucker never got to see. Still, the War Department told families a War Dog couldn't come home after the conflict ended. Children in the home might not be safe. But Uncle Jacob knew who to call. Joe returned home on July 4, 1946. He ran into the backyard during last year's Independence Day picnic.

Tucker wanted to roll over and let the morning rise slowly. It would be over an hour until sunrise. Still, there was something about that particular day, even from its very beginning. Something was in the air. He had a strong feeling this was going to be a great day. Halloween was tomorrow.

The corners of his mouth turned up in a smile as the dog urged him to leave his bed. Joe nuzzled his soft, wet nose up under Tucker's arm. He smiled, popped out of bed, grabbed his Levi's and white t-shirt from the chair where he flung them the night before and followed the dog downstairs.

Where are you going, Joe? He passed Uncle Jacob's large cluttered desk in the front hall. Grandpop was sitting in his Morris chair with his feet up.

"Tucker, would you put more coal on the fire?" His grandfather asked with half closed eyes. Joseph got up every morning at four AM. By the time Tucker came down stairs, it was time for a nap.

"Sure, Grandpop." Tucker hurried on through the dining room, past the stove and new modern refrigerator in the kitchen, but turned before going out to the summer kitchen. "Are ya comin'?" he asked the shepherd. But Joe didn't move and just stood at alert at the back door. Tucker went on down to the basement.

The large round pot-bellied furnace occupied a large area on the left side of the basement. Beefy trunk lines stretch out from the burner like a den of snakes. He took the broad, stubby coal shovel from its spot near the coal room door and shoveled up a scoop of the shiny black fuel. Opening the heavy grated iron door to the coal burner, the few coals that his grandfather shoveled in earlier that morning blazed brightly like beady, orange-red eyes, glaring back at him.

By the size of the fire, it looked to Tucker like Grandpop had only shoveled in one scoop of coal that morning. No wonder the house still had a chill. Tucker scooped up another shovel full and flung it into the furnace.

After putting the coal shovel back in the exact spot Grandpop kept it, he darted past the sweet-peachy-smelling fruit room and up the steps. Joe ran into the summer kitchen, a small room located at the side/back of the house. It was part of the original house before an Amish building crew tore it down to make room for the existing home. Each Monday, Grandpop put a kettle of water on the old wood cookstove, then transferred the hot water to large wash-tubs. The same washing process on Saturdays created bathtubs for weekly bathing. That is unless Tucker fell into the creek or helped

Mr. Kratzen dig up his gladiolus bulbs for wholesale flower distribution. Weekly baths would never be enough for Tucker.

Joe danced in a frenzy, but not because of the backroom. The shepherd dog stood at the locked door to the vast outside and waited impatiently. His destination was in the yard. He seemed to tap dance on the summer kitchen floor as his toenails snapped against the concrete. He wanted out. Now!

When Tucker opened the weather-stained door, Joe darted out into the dim, pre-dawn light. The sun wouldn't be up for another hour and a half. The boy turned on the outside light above the door and glanced around the backyard. The last of the large garden lay nearly empty, almost stripped of all its produce. A few pumpkins waited to fill some of Gramma's delicious pies. It was also time for the black walnut and apple trees to drop their treasurer. Tucker saw nothing outside and started to close the door. Suddenly, his heart leaped in his chest as his eyes caught a glimpse of movement at the base of the tulip tree a few yards from the back door. He jumped inside and grabbed a tighter hold on the doorknob. *Odd. Why did Joe stop barking?* Then from out of the morning shadows, he heard something familiar.

A deep voice teased from beyond the house. "Tucker? You gonna lock me out?"

Tucker squinted as a figure moved toward him. Suddenly, his mouth dropped open, and a smile took over his face. "Sam Treadway? You get in here before I sic the dog on ya."

"Joe?" Sam picked up something from where it lay propped under the tree and stroked the dog's head. "You know me, don't ya, Joe? I only stop by to see Cousin Rebecca once in a while, but Joe remembers." Sam slapped Tucker on the back in greeting and followed him into the house. "You bet ya. Your grandma is one special lady."

"Sam?" Gramma snorted. She stood behind Tucker and laughed. "You come on in here." She grabbed her cousin Sam and gave him a big bear hug. The bearded man had on a buckskin shirt and Levi's. "I'll put the coffee pot on and scramble up a couple of eggs for ya." She opened the door wide and cautioned, "Wipe your shoes. Ya daresn't bring any dry leaves in the house." She brushed small twigs and dried autumn fudduddles from his shoulders. "How long have you been sleeping under that tree?" To Tucker, she whispered, "Get out four cups. You can have some coffee with toast in it if you want to. Your grandpa is in his chair in the living room." She was near giddy as she hurried up the steps to the kitchen. She hadn't seen Sam for many months. He came and went as he pleased. "Sam, why didn't Joseph find you when he swept off the sidewalk? He's been chasing acorns for weeks now. It's his mission to rid the walk of every stumbling nuisance."

"Oh, I don't know. Didn't see him." Sam pulled a large gold watch from his pocket and flipped it open. "I guess I got here 'bout 2 AM. Didn't want to disturb anyone, so I slept under the stars. I do it a lot anyway." He replaced the timepiece in the small watch pocket at his waist. Before going on up to the linoleum floor of the kitchen, Sam removed his old western boots. He placed the tall, hand-tooled high tops by the back door. Sam was a mountain man, but he knew how to live in polite society.

"All of our beds are taken right now, Sam. But I can find some vacant floor to offer you." Gramma grinned. "Inside the house, of course."

"Full house, Rebecca?" Sam smiled as he leaned his Winchester carbine rifle in a corner of the summer kitchen. Rebecca and Joseph Moyer always had room for one more. "Must be this boy that's takin' up so much space." He chuckled as he put his hand on Tucker's shoulder. "I know it's been a while since I've been here, but my lands, boy, you've grown like cottonwood."

"Well," Tucker rummaged through the events of the last year alone. There were real man-making moments. "It's been at least two years." He couldn't take his eyes off Sam's rifle and hoped to inspect it later. It was amazing. From the gold bead sight to the straight-grip walnut stock, it shined.

"Wait a minute." Tucker stopped at the bottom of the steps. "You slept out on the ground since the middle of the night?"

"Have plenty of bedding." Sam adjusted a belt and holster around his hips before going upstairs.

Tucker knew Sam had parked his rifle in the summer kitchen. But where were the pistols that went in the holsters?

"Secret is," Sam continued, "make sure you have enough under ya, between you and the ground. You'll be warm enough."

"Wow." Tucker, mesmerized by this man who lived the life he would have liked for himself, filled his thoughts with high mountains and strong cowboys. In his daydreams, he could almost hear the shout of, "Head 'em up!" as trail hands hitched oxen to freight wagons. They would carry precious cargo between the western edge of Missouri, into Santa Fe, New Mexico, along the Santa Fe Trail. In seconds, he also imagined himself hunting buffalo on the plains, the broad expanse of flatlands west of the Mississippi River tallgrass prairie and east of the Rocky Mountains. Again, he thought, *Wow*!

Gramma led the way up the few steps into the small kitchen. "Sarah Harter is living here now, Sam. Tucker's brother, Tim, is away at the Marines, so Sarah's using his room. I pray for that boy every day." Gramma brought a container to the pitcher pump at the sink and filled it with water. Tucker saw she'd use her new silex coffee pot. Placing the pot on the counter, she added the coffee and poured the water over the grounds.

"I see you got one of those fancy coffeepots, Rebecca." Sam paused a minute. "Ya say Sarah is livin' here, too?"

"She lost everything when that shyster …." Gramma shook her head. "Never mind." She rarely spoke ill of anyone, even someone who cheated a dear relative out of everything she owned. "You know Sarah. Papa's side of the family doesn't speak up about business things." Gramma stopped and plugged in the coffee pot heater.

"I remember Sarah," Sam said as a small grin crossed his face. "We talked a lot when her husband, Steven, was still living. She's a nice person, kinda gentle, and fun to talk to."

Gramma nodded. "Steven died suddenly." She took some eggs from a striped stoneware bowl in the Frigidaire*. She also carried several pieces of thick, sliced bacon to the stove. "Two or three eggs, Sam?"

Sam shook his head. "I don't want to rob you of the food you need for your family, Becca."

"Nonsense, Sam. You're family, too. You'll have three. The hens in the coup were very generous this week."

Sam grinned again at Tucker. "I've learned there's no point arguing with your grandma."

Tucker thought about the Model-A old Noah Dominick gave him last November for his thirteenth birthday. With all the complications Tucker brought to his life at that time, it's a wonder he ever got to drive it again. But that's another story. He did remember, Gramma didn't yell. She just imposed some logical consequences to his lack of follow-through. He didn't argue with her. As Sam said, there was simply no point. The A-Model sat out by the back gate for a few days.

Sam placed some bread on the side doors of the old electric toaster and folded them into the chrome appliance. "I heard Sarah's husband had died. I thought she was living up the street."

"She was living up there, Sam. She had to move from that little place and move in here with us because Ralph Wagoner double-crossed her about the rent." Gramma turned the eggs, stiffened, and rolled her eyes.

Tucker listened. He could see that Gramma felt bad for Sarah. He wondered why she didn't dig deeper into Sarah's plight. To his thinking, some questions still needed answers, and Tucker liked to hear it all. He wondered how a businessman like Gary Wagoner's dad could be dishonest and still be in business.

Grandpop came into the kitchen as Gramma finished frying the eggs. "Sarah told me that Steven's nephew was wise to the situation. Steven's sister's boy, Thomas, said, 'Don't worry about Ralph Wagoner. People have heard many stories about his business dealings. No one will refer any business to him. He's not honest or trustworthy. He's not a man of his word.'"

"Ol' Ralphie Boy?" Sam chuckled. "I remember a straw-haired, dirty-faced boy from a long time ago."

"You know Ralph Wagoner?" Gramma's jaw dropped.

"Oh, do I." Sam helped himself to the coffee. "Ya know, I think I could talk to him about Sarah's situation."

Whispering, Tucker mumbled as he sat. "Well, that conversation should be interesting."

Sam winked at him as he started to sit down.

Joseph laughed as Sam sat beside him and pointed to Sam's holster. "Watch those guns. I don't want you shootin' off my elbow while I eat my breakfast."

"Don't have them in the holster, Joseph. I parked the rifle in the summer kitchen, and my pistols are in my grip."

Tucker's eyes popped. *So that's where they are.* He slapped his hand to his mouth, covering a hidden smile. He wouldn't touch them unless Gramma said he could make a closer inspection. But the fancy hand-guns had always conjured up many dreams of the wild west, like in the novels

Uncle Jacob read, books like *The Ox-Bow Incident.* Tucker saw the movie.

Wow, this really would be a perfect day, including the most exciting daydreams to entertain himself while at school. What could be better than that?

Chapter Two
The Blanket

Tucker ran upstairs and dressed for school. He'd be ready early. Why not? When a fellow is out of bed, he might as well face the morning, regardless of how chilly it is. Rooting through the second drawer of his dresser, he pulled out a long sleeve navy blue sweater. The small mirror behind the door revealed a rumpled line that needed straightening. A push here and a pull there told him he was ready. Taking the upper steps two at a time, he leaped over the final five treads to the entry level below.

Gramma sighed deeply. "Tucker, no jumping in the house."

Tucker thought Gramma sounded tired, and it was only 7:30 in the morning. School started at 8:10, so he had plenty of time to help Sam get his stuff from under the tree, then walk the block and a half to Concord Middle School.

"Sam, I'll help you get the rest of your things out of the backyard." Tucker started for the summer kitchen.

"Tucker?" Christy called from the other side of the door. "Ya up?"

Tucker jerked the door open. "Hi, Christy. I was just going to help Sam a minute. Sam, do you remember—"

"Miss Christmas Tree." Sam bowed like he was meeting Princess Royal, the first-born daughter of the king.

Christy folded her arms across her chest in a huff and glared. Tucker had seen that look often. Christy was not afraid to let others know what she thought about anything and everything.

Tucker winced. "Sam, unless you want to be beheaded by the nearest King's Guard, she goes by Christy."

"Oh, right." Sam apologized with another deep bow. "I just happen to think your full name is beautiful. The Ponderosa Pines in the high mountains of New Mexico are tall and make beautiful Christmas trees. I guess I got you mixed up with them."

"Well…" Christy's pout turned up a little at the corners. "It's okay, just this once. But please, call me Christy."

Tucker's face spread into a big grin. He had never seen Christy soften, even a little, about her name. "Let's go out and help Sam."

Christy followed along behind. "It is good to see you again, Mr. Treadway. I think I saw you the last time you were here. Around Easter, I think. You probably know this Tucker guy better than I do."

Tucker was well aware Sam knew all of the Moyers, including himself and his brother and two sisters. Sam knew all their stories, their plans, their dreams, at least most of them. He returned to Indiana for a visit once or twice a year, just like that late October day in 1947. Gramma regularly wrote long newsy letters, and he followed with sagas of western life in the return mail. She read some of the letters to Tucker. Sam said he marveled at the family's ability to cram so much living into their days. He guessed it was because they spent very little time complaining, leaving more energy for living. Tucker liked that.

From the glow of the backdoor light, Tucker could see more of the yard. As he strolled across the frosted grass, he stared up at the dawning sky. Clouds greeted the day like an eruption of fluff. "Looks like your gear is over there." He pointed to a stash that included a bedroll, a backpack, and other bits and pieces.

As they walked out to the tulip tree, Sam looked farther, to where the dormant half-acre lay at the back of the yard. "Rebecca's garden looks like it was a real wonder. She still has a few pumpkins left out there from the summer."

"Gramma says they should stay on the vine until she gets to them. That way, if they rot before she picks them, the mess will stay on the ground. Makes a little extra fertilizer."

"Can't imagine Becca letting any food go to waste." Sam studied the turned-over rows. "Looks like Rebecca had sweet corn. Some of the stubble is still there. Maybe some morning glories, too. Becca wrote me about them."

When they stopped to pick everything up, Tucker grinned and tapped out a list on his fingers. "Uncle Jacob brings in the big garden tractor and Grandpop turns it all under. It's a family endeavor. Gramma picks out the plants from Gurney's seed catalog; Uncle Jacob and Grandpop till and tend to the ground; Betsy and I gather it all when it's ripe, and; Gramma does the canning."

"A real family project, good for you." Sam reached down and collected a striped blanket in hues* of desert-brown, indigo-blue, and off-white, and began folding it.

"Do you want some help?" Christy offered as she picked up the opposite end of the blanket.

Sam inhaled deeply; his eyes closed. "You know, Christy, I got this blanket from a trading post in Colorado near the base of my mountain," Sam said softly as he smoothed the fold reverently.

"Your mountain, Sam?" Tucker savored every delicious thing Sam said. The thought of Ponderosa Pines in the high mountains already sent Tucker off on a mental adventure.

"Well, not my mountain." Sam shrugged. "The mountains belong to no one but the good Lord. Well ... I guess that's not quite right either. God and I own my small tract of land, and others own theirs. Even the military has a training base on the mountain. But the Native Americans say, the mountain belongs to no one."

"This is a beautiful blanket." Christy folded her end and met Sam in the middle. "I've seen blankets like this in magazines. But never thought I'd see one in person."

Tucker heard the back screen door bang as Joe barked, then darted back into the house. "Yes, Gramma," Tucker shouted in response to Joe's instruction. Gramma sent Joe to remind him that it would soon be time to head off to school.

Sam stepped back a few steps and patted the top of the coarse-spun, woven wool blanket. "Maria Garcia took her son's blanket to the trading post one rainy afternoon. I was in the store at the time and couldn't believe what I was seeing. I said, 'Maria, why would you sell Dakotah's blanket? He'll be chief someday.'"

"Dakotah is no more, Sam," Maria whispered. Her eyes were blank and empty. "He was killed in the Pacific. I don't know how ... he's ... just gone." Sam caressed the blanket as if he were smoothing the hair of a small child.

"Oh, Mr. Treadway, that war ... it just went on and on," Christy empathized. "I'm so sorry to hear about Mrs. Garcia's son's death." She patted the blanket again as if she were touching Dakotah. "We saw so many one- or two-blue stars on flags hanging in windows around Elkhart and Goshen. It showed that a family lived there that had one or two sons in the war."

Tucker looked down at the blanket. "Sam, this is a chief's blanket. Isn't it? I read about those blankets last year. Did a book report on some of the tribes in this area."

"Yes, Dakotah's father is the chief," Sam said. "And Dakotah would have been chief one day. Maria made him a blanket for that important event." Sam unfolded the corner of the blanket again so Tucker could see the pattern. "I told Maria she shouldn't sell the blanket. She would want it one day, as a keepsake to help her remember her son. She said she didn't need anything to remind her of Dakotah."

Christy's voice choked a little. "Sam, sometimes the pain was awful. I'd turn off the radio when the news came on. If Dad wanted to listen, I'd just go to my room."

"You're a good person, Christy. You're both good kids."

Tucker hoisted up Sam's grip. "So, you bought the blanket."

Sam carefully placed the striped wool on top of his bedroll. "No, I told Maria I would give her ten dollars in case she needed some extra money for her other children. She could count it as rent on the blanket. The blanket would always be hers. Maybe someday, she would want it back for one of her other sons. She kissed my hand and handed me the blanket." Sam looked at his hand as if he could still feel Maria's gentle touch on his fingers and patted the blanket again.

Sam and Tucker gathered up all the rest of his gear and started for the door. There was a World War One bag with his changes of clothing, an old Bible, and a leather-bound journal he always carried with him. "Every time I return to the mountain, I take the blanket back to Maria. She touches it and smells the threads. She said it still smells like Dakotah. Tucker, we all have a blanket in our lives, something we have that reminds us of loved ones we've lost. We think we should grow up and get rid of those relics. We punish ourselves because we don't throw them away, and even more if we do. The blanket keeps Maria close to her son."

Tucker thought about it. "What's your Indian blanket, Sam?"

"My Indian blanket?" Sam rubbed his chin as if in deep thought. "I guess I'm one of those who grieve over having clung to nothing."

Tucker had trouble understanding someone who had no attic full of memories. "Sam? You don't cling to anything?"

"Wait!" Sam's eyes brightened as he thought of all he had lost. "No, Tucker. I do have my own blanket. I still have the land ... my farm is near here. I lived there for five years before I went out west after Valerie passed." Sam smiled slowly as a new realization dawned on him. "Maybe I haven't given up everything. I still have my Indian blanket." He started walking toward the house. "I think I understand Maria Garcia. Once you have children, I guess they're always with you. The war took so many of our nation's children. Valerie and I had none. There's no one left."

"Sam, I know you have your memories. You told Gramma and me so many stories." Tucker was sure Sam must have an Indian Blanket besides his farm.

"I know Marie has memories of Dakotah," Sam agreed with a wink. "God gives us children to enjoy for the short days they're here, not to hold them beyond the time God calls them home. I understand that now." He chuckled a little, then added, "It was time for Dakotah to go home. Maria wanted to remember him as he was, not dreaming about who he might have become."

"But she still likes to see the blanket, right? It helps her remember." Tucker thought about the Indian blanket he'll have some day.

"Yes, Tucker, Maria sure does. Time moves real fast. Faster than the arroyos in the valleys of the southwest when the mountain snow melts in the spring. One moment there's a baked, cracked, eroded valley floor. The next moment the water flows so fast and furious down barren tributaries that everything in its path either grows new and green again or is washed away and dies."

Tucker thought some more. "What do you think Grandpop's blanket is?"

"Tucker, Joseph's blanket is his collection of tools. Every chisel and hammer remind him of his work on the railroad, building bridges. They connect him to all the people who need and use his skills today."

Sam smiled. "Becca's blanket is her Bible. She has the birthdays of all the family members in the front. Next to your momma's name are the names of you, four children. There are also the dog-eared passages of scripture Rebecca reads over and over. These are all her blanket. Becca is a woman of integrity and steadfastness. Both of your grandparents are people loved by God."

Tucker knew Sam was right. The tools and the Bible were certainly Grandpop and Gramma's blankets. Then he thought again about his own stripped, chief's blanket. He scratched his head and wondered, what in the world it would be? Then, he knew. *Dakotah is gone, and Mama too. The thought of more people missing is more than I can stand. I guess my Indian blanket is my family, and seeing Bobby again would complete my tribe. If I could spend some time with Bobby, now that would be a perfect day.*

Chapter Three
The Joy of Learning Something New

Tucker hurried into the first-period classroom just as the bell rang. Christy walked to school with Tucker. So, her plaid, wool skirt slid into the chair one row over and two seats up, at the last tick of the clock.

"Well, look," pesky Anna Frederick mocked, "Mr. McBride is here on time. But it looks like you nearly jeopardized Miss Christy Tree's perfect attendance."

"Class, settle down." Jeffrey Callahan, the new eighth-grade math teacher, raised a hand as he took attendance.

The first ten or fifteen minutes of the school day were "homeroom" activities. The teacher counted those present and the number of students who planned to eat in the school cafeteria. When the public address speaker box squawked, everyone finally settled down to listen to the principal's announcements.

"Good morning. First, we have a word from Coach Gray."

"Morning. Today, after school, I've called a special tryout for the boys' basketball team. Several of our team members have Infectious Mononucleosis, and we need additional players. Come to the gym as soon as you can. I know this is Halloween, but Mono doesn't care. You can use the phone in the athletic office to call your parents about the change."

"Thanks, Coach," Mr. Metzger said with a chuckle in his voice. Tucker knew the principal was a great guy who liked a good joke and treated everyone fairly. "That leads into another safety reminder. Mononucleosis has spread to many of our students. Remember, do not share pop bottles or silverware in the cafeteria. Try to avoid using the drinking fountains in the hallways. Our hard-working custodian, Mr. Weaver, does a bang-up job of keeping everything clean and sanitized, but he can't follow everyone. Stay away from the fountains. If you feel extra tired or run a fever, stay home." Principal Metzger paused. "And stay safe out there for Beggars' Night."

While Mr. Metzger spoke to the school body and Mr. Callahan pulled lesson plans from his large, leather briefcase, Tucker used that homeroom time for planning. Sometime that evening, he wanted to go down to the airport. The Midway Airport was one of his favorite places. It wasn't a large international airport, just a little spot owned by Elkhart County. Companies in the area flew in and out of Midway, and flying enthusiasts, who owned an airplane, also called Midway their home. That Halloween, Tucker's friend, Rex Martin, might be taking his plane up. Besides Rex, Walter Crompton was another friend and Sunday-afternoon pilot who owed Tucker an airplane ride. Tucker helped Walter get his Cessna 172 out of the mud some time ago. Then there were activities at home to think through. He hadn't seen Sam Treadway's rifle and a brace of pistols up close yet. He promised Gramma he wouldn't pick up Sam's guns, but he sure wanted to see them. The boy learned his lesson last summer when a bullet grazed his finger.

"Okay, people." Mr. Callahan tapped a pencil on the wooden desk. "Let's get to our discussion for today. We began a unit of study on the Stock Market at the beginning of the school year. We learned large corporations raise money to build their businesses by selling off part of their company. We call each of those small pieces a 'share,' or a 'stock' in the company. The owner receives proof of their share by getting a fancy piece of paper called a stock certificate.

People buy and sell their shares at a place in New York City called the Stock Exchange. We'll continue that unit by bringing in the business section of the newspaper. So far, you've selected your three stocks. Over the past six weeks, you've tracked the rise or fall of the shares in the newspaper." Callahan looked at the front row when a hand went up. "Yes, Anna."

"Mr. Callahan," Anna began as she twisted a curl in the front of her hair. "My mother saves the newspapers. She soaks them in water and rolls them into logs to burn in the fireplace."

"That's a great idea, Anna." Mr. Callahan walked over to the large window, looked out onto the road, and rolled his eyes. "I'm sure she won't miss one sheet of the paper. If you've selected all three of your stocks from that same page, you only need to bring in that one piece of newsprint to track the growth of your stocks."

"Or, track the drop in your stock's value," Yvonne Sherbet, the girl behind Christy, slipped in. "Some people lose a lot of money on the stock market."

Mr. Callahan shrugged. "Of course. Investing in anything can be risky."

Gilbert scooted down in his chair with his long legs sticking out below Yvonne's desk. Tucker always thought Gilbert could be a good basketball player as tall as he was. That is if he could make a basket. Gilbert grumbled, "I wish I had some money to invest."

Mr. Callahan camouflaged a smile as he wiped his chin. "We weren't really going to buy a stock, Gilbert. Our stock unit is a class exercise in buying, charting, and selling."

"Uncle Fred lost his home and his business in the fall of 1929 when the stock market crashed." Yvonne's pout looked like a permanent fixture to her otherwise pleasant expression. "Daddy said I shouldn't learn to use the devil's tool for fast money."

"I wouldn't call the Stock Market the devil's tool, Yvonne. Nor would I call it fast money." Mr. Callahan swallowed then added. "As I remember the story of the loss of Fred Sherbet's plumbing supply business, Mr. Sherbet bought many shares of the Ace Piping Company."

Tucker heard Mr. Callahan drone on about a private limited company. Then Mr. Callahan's voice blurred to a list of, "Blah, blah, blah." Then he said something about the piping company becoming insolvent, and more, "Blah . . . blah, blah."

Yvonne's lower lip protruded like a perch, ready to provide a spot for a late summer bird to land.

Tucker heard some more comments about various relatives of students. Some were successful with investments, and some were not. But mostly, his thoughts wandered off in other directions. Sam Treadway and Maria Garcia's blanket weighed heavily on his mind. He considered possible events at the airport that evening and Halloween the following day. He remembered Sam's arrival and all the adventures he brought. All the while, many other things that stimulated Tucker's curiosity swirled in his head.

"Tucker," Mr. Callahan interrupted his daydreams. "How are your stocks doing?"

"My stocks?" Tucker snapped back into the classroom but had no real idea how to answer. "Well, two are just staying in a flat pattern. But one has shot up a lot."

"Too bad you didn't have real money on that stock." Anna's sassy tone didn't sound sympathetic to Tucker.

"I did."

Mr. Callahan's eyes shot back to Tucker. "You did what?"

"One stock I tracked was a share of RTS Television I bought more than a year ago."

Callahan's eyes blinked as he leaned in Tucker's direction. "Normally, you can't buy just a few shares, Tucker. How did you do that?"

"Gramma's nephew is a CPA and investment counselor. He bought some shares for me, along with his purchases, a little over a year ago. I gave him the money I earned from detasseling corn for several of the farmers around Dunlap. I've been following that company. I can't figure out why it shot up so fast lately, but it did."

Silence hung over the class. Mr. Callahan shook his head in amazement. "Well class, one of our own made real money, green, crisp, spendable money on one of his stocks." He threw his head back and smiled. "It probably grew fast after President Truman made the first Presidential address over the television from the White House on October 5. Everyone wants a TV set in their living room. The stock split 5-to-1 on Monday, October 6. That means each investor received four shares for each they owned, although each with lesser value. If you owned one share, you now have five. Then, on Tuesday, October 7, the price of each stock shot up."

"Wow," Freddie, his best friend, and neighbor gasped. His wide eyes seemed to look at his friend with fresh amazement.

Mr. Callahan stepped behind the desk and checked his lesson plan book. "We will complete this exercise next week. Tucker, you decide then if you want to keep your stock or sell it."

Tucker said nothing. He also didn't bother to add it all up. For Tucker, more of anything was better than some of nothing, just an imaginary investment.

Chapter Four
A Stranger

Tucker left the house, fully intending to walk back to school after lunch. Gramma's lunches had gotten a little skimpier as she got older. Or maybe the truth was, Tucker's appetite had grown as his stature grew. The leftover meatloaf from supper the evening before had made a delicious sandwich. Several handfuls of potato chips from the chip-tin* filled in some of the empty spots in his stomach the sandwich had missed. He liked his grandmother's cooking. But he was still hungry. He took a short detour and crossed the highway to Butch Randolf's Sinclair gas station, next to the grocery. Butch sold more than gas, tires, and sparkplugs.

"Well, hi there, Tucker." Butch looked up from the tire he was wrestling free from its rim. "Aren't you supposed to be in school?"

"I am, sorta." Tucker grinned as he entered the work bay.

"Oh, you're home for lunch. How long 'til you have to be back to school?" Butch stopped and wiped his hands on a blue shop rag.

Tucker checked his watch. "In ten minutes. Gotta hurry."

"Your dad, Sean, was in earlier. He said your brother, Bobby is back in town with his mother."

"You know Bobby?" Tucker was shocked. He began to think the existence of a younger brother was a secret. Maybe even a figment of his imagination.

"Tucker, I've been in business on this corner for over fifteen years," Butch reminded him. "I've known Martha, Sean's second wife since she was a teenager. And Bobby was a little boy when his mom moved them west."

Tucker's mind raced. Bobby was in Indiana again, but school held Tucker captive. That evening was Beggars' Night and the night, jammed full of fun and activities, had no time for brother-hunting. Tucker glanced at his watch again. He'd better hurry.

"No, I didn't know Bobby was in town. Hope I get to see him." He studied the shelves of the glass-front candy case and ended up selecting his usual treats. "I'll have a Heath bar, a Payday, and a Mounds." He stepped behind the counter, slid the case open, and picked out the bars. From his jeans pocket, he pulled out fifteen cents and laid it on the register.

Tucker wolfed down the yummy coconut and chocolate Almond Joy candy bar in what seemed like one bite. Butch's eyes popped, but he knew Tucker. "I don't see how you can do it. It looks like you'd need to chew that bar."

"I chew," Tucker teased back, "enough to swallow."

Butch laughed and shook his head in disbelief. "Monday, Walter Crompton is bringing his work truck in for new brakes. Any chance you could work the drive after school while I'm busy in the bay?"

Tucker heard what Butch said while his eyes stayed focused on the bus that stopped at the corner. He watched a young boy, with his cap pulled down low, step off the bus and headed past the station. *Why does he look so familiar?* "Uh…" Tucker cleared his head. "Sure, I can pump the gas. People will be heading home from work about then." He looked back outside as the sun sent a glare on the window. The boy was gone.

"Great, thanks." Butch opened the cash register and dropped the coins in the nickel compartment. "See you after school on Monday."

"Or before," Tucker added as he opened the door. He started jogging toward the school in the noon-day sun. The middle-school building was only a block away, but he managed to finish the other two candy bars before he burst through the east doors. One was salty and the other crunchy. To Tucker, the important part was not the taste. It was feeling full.

Chapter Five
Four in the House, One in the Bush

After school, Tucker could hear Christy trying to catch up as he hurried out the east door of the school. "Tucker, where are you going?"

"Sorry, Christy." He answered as he hurriedly walked backward while talking to her. "I'll check in at home first, then go over to Winkler's Grocery to see if he needs any chores done."

"Okay. I gotta go home. Mom and I are going into Garland's Department Store. We're getting a baby shower gift for my cousin."

"When will ya get back?"

"In about an hour."

"Come over after supper," Tucker called after Christy before running across the side street beside the school. "I'm going down to the airport later."

Tucker hurried down the gravel alley, kicking up small rocks and sending them flying. Remaining autumn leaves of brilliant orange and crimson, from the yards on both sides of the wide lane, fluttered to the ground. The crisp air invigorated him.

"Hey, Tucker," Freddie Cooper came jogging up behind him. "What ya doing?"

"Gotta chart today's stock market report, then go over to Winkler's Grocery to see if he needs any help."

Freddie trotted beside him for several yards before Tucker turned left into the backyard, and Freddie continued toward home. "Hey, Freddie," Tucker called out, "Christy and I are going to check out the airport after supper. Do you want to come with us?"

"Sure. meet you back here after I eat." Freddie jogged on down the alley to the T intersection, turned, and sprinted in the direction of his house.

Sprinting through the gate, Tucker noticed the garden. It looked like Grandpop had pulled a winter blanket of leaves over it in preparation for the cold weather. In the spring, he would turn the leaves under the soil. Behind Grandpop's workshop was a small flower bed of orange mums. They looked bright and happy against the tall row of shrubs and the green leaves of the lilac bushes. Thick and deep, they provided a windbreak for the yard.

As usual, Joe lay stretched out with his paws in front of him. He always waited there for Tucker to return home from school. But today was different. The minute Tucker stepped into the yard, Joe jumped to his feet and darted over to the hedgerow. There, he stood stiff and straight and unmoving.

"Psst … Tucker." The late October shadows were long across the yard and darkened at the hedgerow. Tucker knew it would be Halloween the next day, but when the bushes began to call to him, that was too much. He started to dash past the spooky evergreens when he heard Grandpop in his workshop. Looking back, Tucker saw that Joe continued to stand alert.

"Psst, psst … Tucker." The tall branches blew in the breeze.

Tucker shot a glance over at the tall hedge but didn't stop. He thought of warning Grandpop but had to admit the question was who would protect whom?

"Tucker McBride," a figure, somewhat shorter than Tucker, stepped out from under the bushes and commanded. "Stop."

"Who…?" At first, Tucker couldn't make out who was the talking garden gnome creeping out from the shadows of the evergreens. Then, Tucker couldn't believe who it was. "Bobby?"

"Yeah, it's me." The boy stepped closer as late afternoon sun rays beamed across his face.

Tucker looked around the otherwise empty yard. Grandpop was still hammering in his shop. "How'd you get here?"

"I took the bus," Bobby said with a skittery expression on his face. "I recognized your house, got off down the street, and walked back. I came down the alley and squeezed in through the bushes." He kept a wary eye on the big German shepherd, but when the boy heard Tucker's grandfather at work in his shop, he suddenly jumped.

"Joe won't hurt you if I'm here, Bobby. What's wrong?"

"Okay," he accepted but fixed his eyes on the dog. "Is there someplace I can hide?"

"Hide? Why are you hiding? I've been hoping to see you for a couple of years. Now you want to hide?" Tucker hadn't seen his half-brother, Bobby, since the younger McBride was five years old. Tucker figured Bobby was a little over eleven now. There he stood, in Tucker's yard, afraid of something. "What's going on? Aren't a lot of people looking for you?"

"Not so you'd notice." His eyes stayed fixed on the top of his shoes. "I've wanted to see everybody here, too. That's why I ran away." Bobby nearly melted himself back into the bushes. "I don't want anyone to see me."

"Not anyone?" Tucker thought for a minute. "Well, sure, I can hide you. But, not until it's dark."

Bobby kept his eyes on Moyer Avenue that flanked the side yard. "What time does the sun go down here in Indiana?"

"Um, a little before six in the late fall." Tucker put his hand in his pocket and began pacing. "Hey," he pulled his Model A car key from his pocket. "You can hide in my

Model A. I'll go in the shop and make sure Grandpop doesn't come out until you get situated."

Bobby's eyes bulged. From where he hid between the bushes, he could see the A Model. "That's your car, Tucker? You're not even fourteen yet."

"I know." Tucker grinned. He loved to present an improbable fact. "A friend, old Noah Dominick, gave it to me for my birthday last year." Tucker motioned for Bobby to wait in the shadow of the bushes while he checked the backyard. "All's clear, now. Wait until I get inside the shop to keep Grandpop occupied, then get in the old Ford."

Tucker heard pounding coming from Grandpop's workshop again. He motioned to Bobby with his finger to his lips. "Here," Tucker handed Bobby the key to his Model A. "Unlock the door, slip in, and crouch down on the floor. It's a coup, so it's not very roomy, but that will have to do until after dark. "I'll go in Grandpop's workshop and make sure he doesn't come out in the yard."

Bobby darted to the side of the workshop as Tucker slipped in through the hand-made shop door. Every tool in Grandpop's workspace was a hand-tool. No saw or drill had an electric cord. The energy to drive a screw came from Grandpop's muscles, regardless of how old he got. Everybody in the neighborhood knew where to borrow a hammer or chisel. The only instruction: *Ya daresn't loss it**.

"Hi, Grandpop. What ya doin'?"

"Makin' a toolbox for your cousin, Jimmy."

"For the cousins? You made one for Harold, too." Tucker knew everything his Grandpop made. He watched every saw cut and hammer strike when he was in the workshop with his grandfather.

"Hope to make one for all you boys." Grandpop didn't look up but ran his wrinkled hand over the smooth surface he was sanding.

Tucker didn't want to think about why his elderly grandfather only *hoped* to make the toolboxes. "You'll do it." Tucker tried to assure himself of his grandfather's ability to work forever. He had to change the subject. "What kind of wood is that frame made out of?"

Grandpop smiled. "That wood is an orange crate, Tucker. I asked Simon Winkler to save all the crates he didn't need."

Tucker noticed the impossible-to-remove paper advertising label on the inside of the crate. "Great idea, Grandpop." Tucker figured Bobby would have gotten to the A-Model by that time. He checked his watch. It was 4:30. "I'll go in and see if Gramma needs help with dinner."

"Okay, Tucker." Grandpop continued to fix his eyes on the task he loved.

Tucker closed the workshop door on his way out. He hurried over to the A Model to check on his stowaway. He called out as quietly as possible, "Bobby?"

"I'm here," Bobby whispered, "folded back and forth like an accordion." The boy, crouched down on the floor, had his right leg folded over the left.

When Tucker saw Bobby in his pretzel pose, he winced. "How long can you stay like this?"

Bobby tried to flip his blond hair out of his eyes but couldn't reach it. His right hand, trapped under his backside, had fallen asleep. "Don't know how long I can last." He wiggled a little. "My left leg is numb already, too."

"I'm going in to have supper. I'll bring you some food after we eat. If you have to use the bathroom, the old outhouse is right there." Tucker pointed to a small wooden structure beside the fence.

Bobby wrinkled his face. "Outhouse? I never used one of those in California. Jack Benny's place even has a bathroom in the pool-house. That's the only yard-john I'm familiar with."

"Jack Benny?" Tucker nearly shouted but caught himself when he heard Grandpop whistling. "You know Jack Benny?"

"Well," Bobby hesitated. "Sorta. I went with Mom to deliver a package. Do you know Mr. Benny?"

Tucker shook his head in disbelief. Did Bobby mean the radio star, Jack Benny, or some neighborhood guy with the same name? "Do you happen to know his wife's name?"

"What?" Now it was Bobby who sounded confused. "Mrs. Benny's name is Mary."

Tucker gulped. Jack Benny, of *The Jack Benny Radio Show,* was a favorite program the family listened to every Sunday night. That Jack Benny's wife is Mary Livingston. "How did you meet Jack Benny?"

"My mom makes complete layette sets for people out in Hollywood. You know, clothes and things for babies: tea shirts, booties, pajamas, quilts—that kind of stuff."

Tucker shook his head again. "Actually, no, I don't know. In my family, we just hand down baby sleepers and cloth diapers to the next cousin." He scratched his dark, wavy hair. "I'm going in. See you in a little while." As he jogged toward the house, a small smile spread across Tucker's face. "Wow, my little brother, another McBride, knows Jack Benny."

Chapter Six
Stuck and Unstuck

Across US 33 from the Moyer home, Tucker popped into Winkler's Grocery Store. "Simon?" Tucker hollered as he threw back the door with the Wonder Bread advertisement painted on the screen.

"Well, hello there, Tucker." Simon saluted. Simon Winkler looked the same day, with his dark blue pants that hung almost to the floor, but not so close he'd trip. A white shirt with rolled-up sleeves couldn't hide the many stains from handling the meat, even though his wife bleached them at every washing. Over it all, he wore a long, white butcher's apron, with a high-placed pocket for his pen. He wore thick-soled black lace-up shoes that eased the pounding his feet took while standing all day. To Tucker's thinking, Simon was the very magazine image of a grocer and butcher.

"Need anything done?" Tucker asked as he scanned the shelves and counter near the door. "I checked your porch and parking area before I came in. The entry looked pretty good."

"Don't need a thing today, my friend," Simon said with the flourish of a royal bow. "But, thanks."

"Your roof still holding? No leaks?" Tucker had crawled around up in the rafters last year and stopped a bad leak.

"No leaks, no drips, no problem." Simon wiped his hands on his heavy, long white butcher's apron.

"Good." Tucker stepped farther into the store. He remembered patching the store roof with pride. "I'll go home and get my homework done. First, Simon, I'd like a little cheese to give me some brain food."

Simon walked to the back of the store and stepped behind the meat counter. Tucker moved more slowly through the store, gawking at the candy counter and the potato chip display as he went.

"How much?" Simon asked, sliding the door in the refrigerated meat display case to the side.

"A quarter pound of cheddar." Tucker watched as Simon removed the large round of cheese from the meat case and carried it to the slicer and scales.

"Always wondered about those scales. They sure look old."

"They are old." Simon laughed. "No need to replace something that still works. Two businessmen made these machines. Edward Canby and Orange O. Ozias lived over in Dayton, Ohio. They purchased the patents to a computing scale someone had just invented. In 1891 the two men organized a company, the Computing Scale Company, where they produced the scales. Mr. Ozias's initials were O. O. O. Doesn't that seem perfect for someone who owned a scale company?"

"That's sharp. Simon, you always come up with the most interesting stories."

Simon laughed and looked at Tucker over his glasses. "Not as many stories as your Uncle Jacob's tall tales and fascinating research."

"That's because he reads all the time and seems to remember everything." Tucker smiled as he shook his head. "After a game one Saturday, I was showing Uncle Jacob the pictures of all the past basketball players Coach Gray put in the display cases in the hall. When Uncle Jacob nearly finished studying every image, he pointed to a photo. "Harold Swanson. There was a picture of Gregory Swanson around there near the beginning of the display. The dates listed under his name said he played twenty-six years ago.

His statistics were almost the same as this Swanson. I wonder if they were related."

Simon stopped and chuckled as his stained, white butcher's apron bounced up and down. "That Jacob. He remembers everything, for sure." Simon wrapped the cheese in white paper and secured it with a string as Tucker stretched up on his toes to see the scales over the counter. "There you are, Tucker. A little over a quarter-pound."

"Well, Simon, it looks well packaged to me." Tucker placed the cheese package on top of his books. "See ya tomorrow." Tucker put twenty-five cents on top of the meat counter, "Thanks, Simon." Tucker started for the door when he heard Simon's phone ring.

Tucker could hear the store-side of the conversation. "Afternoon, Mildred. What? Sure, I think. Wait." Simon held the receiver away from his ear. "Tucker?"

Tucker turned before he got to the door. "Need something, Simon?"

"It's Mildred Custer. She has six dozen sugar cookies, all iced and decorated with Halloween pumpkins, to bring to the store. The batch she sent last week smelled sweet and moreish*. But her car won't start. Is there any way you could safely ride your bike out to her place and pick them up for me? I can't get away from the store. We're open late tonight because of Halloween. Some people run in here to pick up a few things as they take their kids around for Beggars' Night."

Tucker started to speak, then smiled. "I can get them for you, sure."

"Great. I'll call your grandmother and let her know you're going to run an errand for me. It shouldn't take you very long."

Tucker darted out the door in the direction of his backyard. "Yes...yes." He smiled every step of the way to the A Model.

The dry fall leaves scattered all over the ground, crunched and crackled as he walked. The autumn aroma of burning leaf smoke filled the air from a neighboring yard. "Bobby?" he called out in a hoarse whisper.

"Yeah?" came a voice from inside the parked antique Ford.

"Want to go for a ride?"

"Sure," Bobby suddenly regained energy as he unwound himself from the floorboard of the old car.

"Stay down," Tucker warned, "until I get the car out of the yard."

Tucker jumped in, put the key in the ignition, and started the car. At the putting sound of the engine, Grandpop stuck his head out of the workshop door and hollered, "Where ya goin', Tucker?"

"Mr. Winkler asked me to run out to Custer's farm and bring the cookies Mrs. Custer made to sell this evening at the store. Her car won't start."

"Ja, Tucker. You hurry along." Grandpop went back into his workshop. From the sound of hammering, Tucker knew he had gone back to work.

As Tucker pulled out of the drive, Bobby wiggled up onto the seat. "How far is it, Tucker? Wow. I can't believe you can drive this thing."

"Just a few miles." They bounced along the road until they came to the Yeager Meat Packing Company. A driver maneuvered his huge truck backward down the long unpaved drive, aiming the vehicle toward the loading dock. The truck gears ground and scraped as the driver winced.

"Can you go around, Buddy?" the trucker asked as his arm hung in limp surrender out the window of the truck cab.

Tucker checked over his shoulder. There was a small field access road across the street from the meatpacker. "I think I can." Tucker pulled into the little lane to give himself more space to make the turn. The tires slipped in the mud and sludge of the open field, recently harvested of its corn.

"Uh-oh," Bobby moaned.

"It'll be all right. I can get us out," Tucker said confidently. He turned the steering wheel every which way, but the tires only sunk more deeply into the gunk and slimy mud. "Maybe if I back up a little and get a longer, head start on the road, I can run us back onto the pavement."

"That makes sense," Bobby agreed. Maybe it would have been the thing to do if the field was dry and only needed a little bit of professional driving.

But the field was far from dry. It had been raining for several days before the Halloween weekend. While Tucker had learned to drive the Model A, he was not an Indycar driver. It would be much easier to get tire traction at the "brickyard" on race day than in the dark, soaked earth of the farm field.

Tucker studied the field over his shoulder. The entire ten-acre plot stretched out in deep trenches, or furrows, left by much larger tractor tires. "Maybe we could get out of this globby field if you pushed."

"Me?" Bobby complained. "Get out of the car in this mess? I thought you were going to get us out of here."

"I will." Tucker smiled and turned the wheel again. "I'll be the one driving."

Bobby laughed, pounding his hand on his chest. "And I'll be the one providing all the power."

Tucker put the car in reverse gear and allowed it to roll back farther into the acreage. "I can get a rolling start from here." Several yards down a slight slope, he stopped the car and put it in gear. Slipping and sliding, the old A Model could not grab the traction necessary to pull the small car out of the muck. Rather than creep forward, the Ford lost ground. After the shifting of gears, and a lot of breath-holding, Tucker's little A. It stopped two yards back from where he started.

Then he remembered what Uncle Jacob did when his car was stuck in the snow the previous winter. He "rocked" the vehicle back and forth, slipping it from forward, into reverse, and then back again to forward several times. The black coup inched forward, then lost ground again as the rumble seat swerved in the mud. "Now, don't worry. I can solve this." Suddenly, Tucker heard someone tapping hard on his side window.

"Sorry, Buddy," the truck driver apologized. "There wasn't any way for you to get around me. Guess I was in a hurry. I picked up the sausage and hams for the Markham Market chain. Let me push you out."

"Thanks." Tucker's grip relaxed on the wheel. "You'll get awful muddy back there."

"That's okay. I wore my high-top boots today." The man's scowl had relaxed to a grin.

Tucker glanced down at the man's boots that came within inches on his knees. "Great pair of timber boots."

"Thanks. I'm going to close the rumble seat," the trucker said, stomping through the mud. In the back of the car, he reached in and released the latch. That allowed the back of the seat to fold down like a trunk lid, which placed the seat cushion inside. "Okay, Buddy, I can push you now. Press down, slow-like, on the gas."

With the shove from behind and Tucker's foot pressing gently on the accelerator, the Model A gripped the ground. As the car crept slowly, Tucker bounced up and down in the driver's seat. "The A is climbing like a mountain goat," he shouted.

Safely back on the road, Bobby exhaled deeply and teased. "I thought you were the one who'd get us out."

"I am. I drove, and we're out, aren't we?" Tucker reached over and bopped his brother on the knee. "Now for the real mission. Cookies!"

Mildred Custer lived at the next farm. White lettering on the red barn read, "115 miles to Wrigley Field." The lane was short and smooth. "Now, this, Bobby is a country lane, not a field access path."

As they turned into the gravel drive, Bobby asked, "You didn't say anything about calling our dad to come and help us. If I had been in that mess, I would have called Roger, my step-dad, to come and help me out. He would come in a snap."

"Dad is around a little," Tucker nearly whispered. "We usually call him Sean when he's not around. Betsy and I go to Dad's every once in a while, more often when we were younger. And he came to Toledo last year when some friends and I overshot Goshen and found ourselves at the end of the line. He drove us all home. That was nice. Sometimes I see him in Garland's Department Store where he works."

Bobby spoke with a whisper. "That's better than nothing."

They sat for a minute in Custer's barnyard. Tucker broke the silence. "I always wished he could make it to some of my ball games. Last year, he told me he came to them a lot but sat high up in the stadium so no one would see him."

Bobby shook his head in sad disbelief. "Why did he hide?"

Tucker didn't like to let others in on family pain. "When Mother died, my grandparents blamed Sean for not taking care of her better. He didn't even want to call the doctor and insisted, "She'll be fine." Then, there was a time at the church when I was a baby and Sean came into an evening service. He smelled of alcohol and tried to take me with him. Some of the men of the church had to throw him out." He pointed to Mrs. Custer as she came out her kitchen door carrying a large box. Tucker wrapped up his story with a few words. "There's been a lot of pain in the family."

"Afternoon, Tucker," Mildred greeted. "Thanks for coming out to pick these up." She looked through the window at the small interior. "Where will I put them?"

Tucker hopped out, came around, and pulled the handle that raised the trunk lid, the back to the rumble seat. "We got in a little mud," he said with an embarrassed laugh. "But it should be clean inside here."

Mrs. Custer placed the box on the seat, handed Tucker a small paper sack, and wiped her hands on her flower-covered apron. She wore a pair of Mr. Custer's scuffed wingtip shoes and bobby socks. She saw Tucker smile at her choice of footwear. "They're comfortable while I'm baking all day." She chuckled. "I really don't care what others think." Pointing at the sack, she added, "Thanks again. The four cookies in the little sack are for you and your friend. Now, I'm going to run back inside. It's cold out here."

"Yes, Ma'am," Tucker said as he held the sack near his nose. The sweet smell of sorghum with a dash of cinnamon escaped from the bag. "Thanks."

To turn around, Tucker drove in a circle around the barnyard, then headed out the lane and back toward Simon's grocery. As the farmland passed outside, Tucker opened the sack. He pulled out a pumpkin-shaped, iced sugar cookie and offered one to Bobby. "Life is good, isn't it, Bob? We got stuck in the mud; I got us out; we did Mrs. Custer a favor, and we got a couple of cookies as a reward."

Bobby teased as he reminded him, "Yeah, but it was the trucker who pushed us out."

"Yep," Tucker agreed with a laugh as he reached for his second cookie. "But I was the one driving."

Chapter Seven
A Good Reason to Drive the Model A

Tucker came back into Dunlap just as the Moyes' next-door neighbor, Mrs. Stuart, reached up to the clothesline and removed another clothespin. She pulled the last four pins that kept a large, white sheet from blowing off onto the ground, folded the bedding, and placed it on top of the wicker laundry basket.

Tucker smiled when he saw her out in the sunshine. "Mrs. Stuart had her first cold earlier this week and stayed in the house," he told Bobby. "It's good to see her outside."

Bobby watched Adele Stuart rest the top of the sheet on the basket as she folded the cotton bed covering to make sure none of it touched the ground. "Are you apologizing for Mrs. Stuart?" Bobby asked with a curled-up lip. "She got her laundry done four days later than usual.?"

"I'm not apologizing for her. I'm explaining. Mrs. Stuart's hard work needs no apology." At the corner, Tucker crossed the road.

Simon must have seen them coming and stepped out of the grocery. The afternoon air was getting cooler. He was still putting his arm in the sleeve of a dark sweater. "Tucker, picking up these cookies for me was great. Your next half-pound of cheese is on me."

"Thanks, Mr. Winkler." After delivering the tasty treats to the store, Tucker drove around to the backyard at his house, where he left Bobby hiding on the floor of the car. Jogging up to the house, Tucker popped inside through the summer kitchen.

With surprising excitement, he spread his math homework out on the dining room table, unwrapped the cheese, and broke off a bite. Recently, math homework had been fun. He liked studying the stocks. When he first bought the one share in 1946, the United Mine Workers of America went on strike from April to December. The strike affected twenty-six states and spread to other industries as well. Then, the market started to move up. He even liked plotting the progress of his three stocks on graph paper, the one he bought in 1946 and the two he chose at school. "Gramma, where is the newspaper?" He tore off another piece of cheese and stuffed it in his mouth.

"Next to your grandpa's chair," she called from the kitchen. "Don't cut it or mess it up. Jacob hasn't seen it yet."

Tucker turned to the Stock Market results page and ran his finger down the columns. Once he found RTS Television and the other two stocks, he jotted down the closing figures and plotted them on his graph paper. Quickly finishing his homework, he finished off the cheese as well, wadded up the wrapper, and shoved it deep into the waste paper basket. Gramma's little silky terrier dog, Tiny, snatched up anything that smelled like food, so Tucker pushed it down far enough so Tiny wouldn't be able to pull it out and tear it up. Tucker took his books up to his room, came back down taking two steps at a time, and made a flying leap off the final four treads. He felt warm, temporarily full, and satisfied inside. He was happy to set his mind on his homework and glad to complete it.

The sweet, toasty smell of Gamma's cornbread was the first clue to supper. It would be one of Tucker and Uncle Jacob's favorite meals – great northern white beans and ham, with golden, sweet cornbread on the side. Tucker wondered how he could get some of the food out to Bobby. The family usually cleaned up every crumb, and now they had two additional people around the table, Sam, and Sarah.

Sarah came into the room, her hands on her hips. "Well, it looks like supper is ready. Why didn't you wake me, Rebecca? I would have helped." Even fresh from a nap, Sarah's auburn red hair still hung in the same wavy curls that framed her face.

Sam looked up as Sarah sat down beside him. Sunlight streamed through the front window, sending sparkling rays around Sarah. Tucker saw Sam blush and look down at his silverware. When Sam's smile twitched, Tucker nearly choked on his swallow of milk. It looked like Sam was doing battle with his face. Sam couldn't stifle a silly grin that appeared to take control. It seemed to Tucker as if Sam had never before seen Sarah. Why was this time different? Sarah blushed, too.

Tucker knew that Gramma noticed the exchange when she brought the warm cast iron skillet and wooden trivet to the table. The hot pad around the handle nearly slipped in her hand. First, she put down the trivet Grandpop had carved out of wood he saved from the trunk of a cherry tree that blew down in a storm. The outer edge was square with an intricately carved sunburst pattern in the center.

Tiny would have been very pleased if some food had fallen on the floor. The little dog yapped a lot while Gramma fixed the food but had learned to stay quiet when the family gathered at the table. She'd lap up a little spillage quickly in silence. If not, she would suffer banishment to the summer kitchen, the consequences of noisy behavior. And it might have been Joe's job to herd her there.

"Tucker, would you bring in the kettle of ham and beans?" Gramma asked as she cut the cornbread into pie-shaped pieces. She'd baked it in the cast iron skillet the hour before.

Out in the kitchen, Joe waited with patient determination. "It's still hot, Joe," Tucker said as he stroked the dog's head. "I can see steam coming from the ham bone, boy." He grabbed two potholders and placed them around the handles of the large cast-iron kettle that sat on the back burner of the old wood-burning Wedgewood stove. The soupy ham and beans sloshed back and forth in the pot. Tucker saw how full it was and carried the kettle carefully into the dining room.

Joseph rested his hands on the arms of his dining room chair and waited for the meal to begin. Sitting there calmly, he seemed oblivious to the feelings between Sam and Sarah that hung in the air like humidity on a hot Indiana day.

"Sam," Joseph picked up his coffee cup and sipped a little. "I'm glad you're here. We're having a parade of little hobgoblins tomorrow for Beggars' Night. I'm in charge of pulling the junior choir bleachers out of the church's storage room and putting them up in the parking lot. Some folks from outside the neighborhood are coming over. They want to see all the ghosts and cowboys parade by in their Halloween costumes."

"Sure, I'll help," Sam agreed. "Becca," he marveled when Rebecca put a ladle-full of beans into a bowl, "that looks wonderful."

"Still running?" Rebecca whispered.

"Huh?" Sam startled.

Huh, Tucker echoed but only in his head. Something was going on at the table. He wasn't sure he understood it. So, he decided to ignore it.

Gramma just smiled. "Tucker, call your sisters to the table, please. They're tarrying."

Tucker hopped up and went over to the foot of the stairs. "Betsy, Carolyn … supper."

The table filled as the girls and Uncle Jacob all joined in. Jacob sat beside Sarah, and the girls took their seats on the other side of the table next to Tucker. Joe stretched out on the floor beside Tucker. Grandpop sat at the head of the table.

"Mother," Jacob smiled when he saw the cornbread, "this is my favorite."

Tucker hesitantly reached for the cornmeal bread and quickly looked at Gramma. She nodded okay as he put a piece on his plate. While all that silent movie nonsense played out between Sam and Sarah, Tucker folded his napkin around the second piece of pie-shaped cornbread and concealed it in his lap.

"Grandma," Betsy complained. "Tucker has two pieces of cornbread."

"There's plenty. I have another skillet-full out in the kitchen." Gramma didn't even look at Tucker but smiled again at Sam.

Tucker saw Sam peek at Sarah from the corner of his eye. Sam had the silliest grin. *Are they kids?* Tucker wondered.

Rebecca whispered in Sam's ear. "Aren't God's little surprises a hoot?"

What surprises? The side of Tucker's mouth turned up in befuddlement. *I don't see anything that's surprising,* he thought. He looked down at Joe and rolled his eyes. The dog tilted his head as if he found the discussion taxing.

"Did you get all your homework done, Tucker?" Gramma glanced at him while she ladled beans into the other soup bowls and placed the bowls on small plates.

"Mother, this is very good." Jacob swooned over his first bite of cornbread.

"I put sugar in it. With the war over, I can get all the sugar I want. No more rations."

Tucker shrugged. "I just had a little stock charting to do." It suddenly occurred to him it was math homework that excited him.

Grandpop reached for Tucker's hand as they all gathered as one family. Some put down their spoon as they bowed, joining him in the grace. He finished with, "Thank you, Lord, for the family and the bounty of sugar and food.

And hold our Tim in the palm of your hand." He put his napkin in his lap and tasted the golden bread. "We didn't have it so bad. We had so many people in the family our ration allotment was enough for Ma to continue to make pies."

"Pie?" To Tucker, a large slab of pie was the main course of any meal.

"Ja," Tucker, "there's peach. I opened a quart jar of peaches I put up last year."

Beautiful peaches, sweetened in the sugar Gramma talked about—ah. Tucker thought of his big brother in the Marines. Tim was a lover of peach pie.

"Stocks?" Carolyn jumped into the conversation again. "I remember charting some stocks when I was in the eighth grade. Gabriel has stocks. When we get married, he said he's going to buy a few more. I know it's hard to make money in stocks. You have to choose carefully."

"I did." Tucker broke off a piece of the cornbread and dunked it in the beans.

"You did what?" Betsy's spoon dropped into the bowl.

"I made money on one of the stocks I bought." Tucker didn't look up from his hot, steamy bowl.

"There ya go, Tucker," Betsy sighed deeply, her shoulders drooped nearly to the table. "You're lying again."

Tucker pounded the end of his spoon on the round oak table surface. "I am not."

"No arguing at the table." Gramma was firm about that. "Tucker is doing an exercise in school in which they *pretend* to buy stocks. Now, let's eat."

Tucker opened his mouth to defend his argument, but he decided against it. Let Betsy think whatever she wants.

When the family all had their mouths full, and the dining room was silent for a minute, Sarah jumped in. "I have an announcement." She put down her spoon.

"Ja?" Gramma stopped and listened.

Sarah refolded the napkin in her lap. "Sharon Snyder, one of the elementary school teachers, is going to have a baby. I interviewed for her job today."

"Sarah!" Sam's joy was exploding on his face.

Tucker didn't know why Sam was so happy. He wasn't going to teach school.

"Oh, Sarah," Gramma encouraged her. "I know you will get the job. I've prayed that God will fulfill His plan for you."

Tucker didn't know why anyone would want to be a teacher. Most days, Tucker wanted out of school. While he ate, he decided he'd have to get his mind off class lectures, homework, and the teachers' no-talking rule. Tuck thought for a minute. "Hey Sam," he nearly shouted with excitement. "Did you bring your pistols?"

"Tucker," Gramma cautioned, "those are dangerous weapons."

"Ma, he just wants to look at them." Grandpop didn't look up as he broke off another piece of cornbread.

Tucker knew Grandpop learned to handle a gun when he was young. He also knew Gramma was well aware of that. He had heard Grandpop talk about it often when Gramma was nearby. Grandpop had told stories in great detail about his parent's farm-home in the hills around Burks County, Pennsylvania. The hills were alive with rabbits, wild turkeys, and deer.

"Is it alright if I show the boy if he doesn't touch them, Becca?" Sam was respectful of the rules Joseph and Rebecca had for their grandchildren. "I do love bringing the kids a new experience from time to time."

"If he doesn't touch them …" Rebecca said no more.

Sam wiped his mouth on his napkin. "Later this evening, I'll show you, Tucker. You and I both will obey your grandmother."

That settled it. For a brief moment, the family was quiet as they savored their dinner. Then silence hovered over the table until Gramma brought in the pie. With eight people to share in the peach deliciousness, each piece would be smaller than usual.

Tucker's eyes grew. "I'll cut it for you, Gramma."

Gramma smiled a knowing smile. "You know the rule. The one who cuts the pie gets the last pick of the pieces."

"Never mind," he said, shaking his head in positive determination.

As he watched Gramma cut the pie, Tucker kept his eyes on the bean pot. After everyone had their second helping, he offered, "I'll take the kettle out to the kitchen for you, Gramma."

"Thank you, Tucker."

With just one-eighth of a piece of pie on his plate, Tucker nearly finished it in four bites. Wiping his mouth, he hurried to the kitchen with Bobby's piece of cornbread balanced on top of the kettle and Joe at his heels. Tucker pulled a large coffee mug from the cabinet, filled it with beans, grabbed another spoon, and hurried out to Bobby in the backyard as the sun began to dip westward. Tucker smiled as he remembered the hymn, *Day is Dying in the West*. He grinned. To him, the day wasn't dying. It was collapsing with exhaustion under the weight of all the activities Tucker managed to cram into it.

Chapter Eight
Always a New Experience

"I'll be back later, Gramma." Tucker pulled his red and black plaid jacket from the hall tree near the side door. Nineteen-forty-seven would be the second winter for the coat. It was beginning to feel tight under the arms and across the shoulders. More of his wrists stuck out every day. Tucker held the jacket up and studied it for possible tears.

"Oh no." He found a small rip, but that wasn't going to stop him. A careful inspection of several of his shirts and other clothing would testify to Tucker's ability to fix them himself.

In a small area off the dining room, in front of the west-facing windows, sat Gramma's treadle sewing machine*. Gramma polished the walnut cabinet every week. It had two drawers down both sides of the machine where she stored thread, needles, and small scissors. Tucker pulled back the hinged cover and raised the Singer sewing machine from its storage space beneath the desk-like top of the cabinet. He checked the lower bobbin thread. *What color? Good.* He added a top spool of black and wound it through the machine.

Seated on Gramma's short stool, he placed the under-arm seam onto the throat plate, lowered the presser foot, turned the handwheel on the right toward him, and pumped the treadle on the bottom of the machine cabinet, and started stitching. The faster he pumped, the faster the needle went, so the quicker the seam closed.

"Tucker?" Christy called from the side porch that faced Moyer Avenue. She tapped gently on the door. "Tucker?"

He turned the jacket around to sew back over the same seam, making a treadle machine's version of a knot, and put his arm in his sleeve. *There's no hole, but it's a little tighter*. He stepped over to the side door and jerked it open. "Come on in while I finish getting my coat on."

Christy stepped inside and rubbed her hands together. "It's getting cold already this Halloween evening. I saw Freddie coming up the street, probably heading here." Christy pulled her collar up around her neck. "It sure smells good in here."

"Gramma fixed ham and beans. They were super." Tucker fastened his jacket. "We had cornbread too. It was sweet and perfect."

Christy turned toward the door. "What ya gonna do'?"

"I see Freddie." Tucker stepped farther out onto the porch, looked down past the Stuarts' house, and motioned for Freddie to come along. To Joe, he commanded, "Stay boy."

Freddie jogged up. "What are you guys up to?"

"I'm going over to the airport and see what's going on." Tucker started walking around the side yard, back to the Model A. A goldfinch flew overhead. Tucker smiled as he remembered the stories of his mother's bright yellow canary that she greeted every morning.

"You gonna drive the Ford?"

"Yep. It'll be tight, but we'll make it." Tucker stopped at the car and whispered. "Bobby?"

"Bobby?" Christy and Freddie repeated in unison as they looked at each other. "Bobby?"

Tucker looked at his friends seriously. "Now ... you two have to swear you won't tell anyone about Bobby."

Christy stepped back. "Tucker, I don't swear about anything. But, if you want me to keep a secret, I'll keep it. Who is Bobby?"

Tucker opened the old car door. "Bobby, it's just us. Come on out."

Christy and Freddie watched as a boy, a few years younger than each of them, unfolded himself from the floor of the Model A. His cheek was red where it lay against the floorboards all morning.

"This is Bobby McBride," Tucker paused and added, "my half-brother. He's run away, and I haven't found out why."

"Bobby McBride?" Freddie nearly squealed. "The one-and-only Bobby McBride? The same one we rode the rails last summer looking for him?"

"The very one," Tucker pointed with both hands like a sideshow barker encouraging those around to view a member of the menagerie.

Christy didn't pick up on the *who* as much as the *what*. "Runaway?" Christy's brow furrowed. "That sounds like Taffy Bean* all over again."

Bobby's mouth flew open. "Taffy Bean, the movie star? She lives in Hollywood with all the rest of the movie people, not Indiana."

"Yes." Tucker held up his hand. "That was last year, Bobby. We'll talk about it later. It seems like a lifetime ago."

Christy folded her arms across her coat. "Let's just say we helped her go home, not run away from there. Enough said."

Bobby nodded. His voice lowered. "I haven't seen Tucker or Tim and their sisters for five or six years. I haven't seen my dad since then, either. Mom always told me Dad died in the war, and I have no brothers and sisters. But I remembered a family here in Dunlap. Mom and I came into Goshen from California on the bus. We're staying at my aunt's house. Aunt Helen told me yesterday, 'Of course you have an Indiana family.' She said, 'Your dad has married again, and they've just had a baby. Your half-brother, Tucker, has two sisters, cousins, and more family and friends.'" Bobby hung his head and whispered. "In California, I only have my mom and step-dad. Here, I have aunts and uncles from mom's family and all their neighbors here in Dunlap." Bobby looked at each face staring back at him. "Please, give me some time to be here. Before we moved west, Elkhart County was my home, too. Maybe I could stay through tomorrow, so I can get to know everyone. I just want to spend time with you, Tucker. I'll have those memories forever."

Christy closed her eyes. "Bobby, your mother is probably scared to death. Think about it. She might think almost anything has happened to you."

"I know, but this is the only way. She'll make me go back to Aunt Helen's right away. If she can say, Dad is dead, I don't think she'd let me see him."

"Okay with you guys?" Tucker asked the other two. He knew Bobby was right. Tucker had wanted to connect with Bobby for a long time. He almost made it a year ago, around the time of his birthday, before the Taffy Bean experience and their detour. "I know Gramma would say Bobby would have to go back right away. She'd worry about his mother."

"Okay, let's go to the airport," Freddie said as he looked at the Model A. "But how? There's a lot of us."

Christy pointed to each one and then to the car. "A coup with a rumble seat. Four people – hum."

"Let's see ..." Tucker studied the arrangement for a minute.

Freddie raised his hand. "I get the back. I have a hat, and I'll pull up my collar. I've always wanted to ride in a rumble seat."

Bobby tipped the bill of his ball cap. "I have a hat. I get the rumble seat, too."

"Okay," Tucker rubbed his hands together, then stuck out a hand in Bobby's direction. As Bobby handed over the key, Tucker introduced him. "Bobby, this is Freddie. Freddie, this is my brother, Bob."

After they all said, "Glad to meet ya," and gave hearty handshakes or slaps on the back, Christy joined Tucker in the front seat. When the key turned, the old Model-A Ford made a putt, putt sound in a soft puh-puh-puh rhythm out onto Moyer Avenue. Tucker turned right toward the small neighborhood airport using the back roads since he didn't have a driver's license. The airport was a favorite spot for most boys of almost fourteen. And Tucker was sometimes able to bum a plane ride with someone who owed him a favor. A year ago, Tucker helped Walter Crompton get his plane back to the airport for inspection. Walt said he "owed" Tucker a ride. Besides, there was always *stuff* going on at the airstrip and in the small hanger.

Christy held onto the door handle as Tucker turned the corner. A ride in the A Model was a bumpy but fun ride. "It's great you finally got to see Bobby again."

Tucker didn't take his eyes from the road. "Yeah ... but it feels funny."

Christy nodded. "Kinda like, you've been on a scavenger hunt for years, then the prize pops out and says, 'Here I am.' Where's the fun in that?"

"I guess the fun of the search was a big part of it." Tucker looked ahead to where an airplane flew low over the street as it came in for a landing. "But you're right. Seeing Bobby again is great. I guess I'm not sure I know what to say to him."

"Say? Tucker, I don't think he wants to say anything. I think he just wants to spend time with you."

"Good. I can do that."

"Besides, you talk all the time. There won't be any shortage of words if that's what you're worried about." As she watched out the window, they turned onto the rough, grass field of the airport. "What's that?" Christy pointed to a piece of machinery off to the side of the runway.

"That's the roller they use to smooth out the runway." Tucker pulled the Ford over near the tractor-like machine with the giant, heavy roller attached to the front.

Christy looked toward the hanger. "Looks like there's nobody around." Checking the sky, she added, "It's getting darker."

"Many of these pilots fly at night. Guess this is just one of those slow days. I was hoping to see a couple of guys, maybe Walter Crompton."

"Mr. Crompton is an electrician, Tucker. When did he learn to fly an airplane? Some say he stuffs his panel truck so full of switches, wires, and electrical stuff, he would treat a plane the same way. The plane would be too heavy to take off." Christy watched as Tucker started down to the area near the hanger.

"Any guy who can drive a car can fly an airplane." Tucker summed it all up. "Men take to the sky."

Christy bristled. "Men aren't the only pilots. There were WASPs – the Women's Airforce Service Pilots during the war. They delivered airplanes all over the country."

"I know." Tucker realized Christy was right. "Milly Miller flies out of this airport regularly."

"Milly Miller?" Christy started to get out of the car. "Milly Miller, Stephanie's mom?"

"Yep. I think Mrs. Miller might have been one of those WASPs you were talking about." Tucker removed the key and looked out the windshield at the runway roller. "I always wanted to check it out, and it's big enough for us all to get on."

"Tucker …" she deliberately stretched out his name. Christy knew Tucker well enough to realize the roller-thing could be a problem.

The boys piled out of the rumble seat, holding their ears, and pulling their jackets closely around themselves.

Bobby shook his head in mock shivers. "It's colder in Indiana than it is in California."

Tucker laughed. "Oh, it gets a lot colder than this."

"What we doin'?" Freddie looked around at what might have caught Tucker's eye. It had to be something nearby. That was what usually grabbed Tucker's attention.

Tucker walked over to the roller and kicked the tires like he was buying a good used car. "Always wanted to see this up close. Glad there's nobody around."

Bobby followed Tucker and gave another poke at the tire. "What is it? They don't have any of these things on the beaches at Malibu."

"It's a ride-on machine for rolling the runway to make it smooth. Since it's a dirt and grass runway, the groundskeeper has to roll it often, so the airplanes are safe to land and take off." Grinning, Tucker reached up and took the steering wheel of the odd-looking piece of machinery.

"Not again!" Christy moaned. "Not another Tucker-shenanigan?"

Bobby climbed on with a grin so big it covered his face. He stood beside Tucker, then Freddie jumped on the other side.

"Okay, okay." Christy tried to mask a broad smile. She wiggled her foot onto a spot on the side where she could step up, grab Bobby around the waist, and hang on.

Tucker only had to look once to see the key was in the ignition. "Wonder why…?" He didn't even hesitate. Reaching down, he casually turned it on. The ride-on ground smoother lurched forward with a jump while all hung on with a scream and a laugh.

As Tucker moved the roller forward, the machine popped and banged across the gravel drive toward the runway, pop, pop, pop. Suddenly, porchlights and barnyard beacons at neighboring homes and farms flipped on.

The four roller *experts* laughed so hard, Christy slipped from the tiny platform and landed on the ground.

Howling in hilarity, she bent from the waist in a loud and boisterous laugh.

Tucker laughed until it was hard to reach the key. There was something semi-sacred about evening quiet time in Dunlap. He quickly managed to grab the key on a bouncing rebound and turned it off. "Let's go," he hooted as he headed back to the car.

All jumped into the Model-A. As soon as Tucker's jeans hit the seat, he started the engine. When the boys climbed in the back and Christy got into the front, they retraced their way back to the streets around Dunlap. Tucker dropped Freddie off at his house and Christy at hers. Bobby jumped in the front with Tucker as they drove the few blocks to the Moyer house.

Tucker pulled into the alley, his usual spot in the yard. They sat there for a minute. "I'm glad you're here, Bobby."

The boy stared out the front windshield in silence. "Me too, Tucker. Today is the best day of my life."

Chapter Nine
A Safe Place to Sleep

Tucker led Bobby through the backyard to the big tree next to the summer kitchen. Silently, he demonstrated how to jump, hoist, and flip himself up into the tree. Joe stood at the base of the maple tree, motionless yet alert, and seemed to supervise the unusual entrance into the home. By then, the dog's friendship extended to the boy who seemed so much like his Tucker.

With Bobby right behind him, Tucker reached for the antenna cable Uncle Jerry installed when he had his ham radio in the Moyer home. Up the boy climbed until he got to his bedroom window that he had unlocked that morning. He thought there'd be more times in the future like this. Swinging through the tree branches to enter his room would be easier than walking through the first-floor door. Tucker tugged on the bedroom sash lift, but the window didn't budge. He pulled on the metal lift again. Tucker smiled and mouthed to Bobby; *Gramma locked it.*

"Now what?" Bobby whispered.

Tucker grinned, reached above the window, stepped on the sill, and grabbed the attic window above him. With a push, it swung open. Tucker pulled himself up and inside. He quickly turned, grabbed Bobby's hand, and pulled him up and through the attic window.

The nearly full moon brought a flood of light into the attic where Gramma and Grandpop stored the family's history. Trunks and boxes lined the eaves. Tucker had been to the bottom of them many times. Grandpop had installed a rod along the wall where Gramma hung the costumes Margie, Tucker's mother, wore for a Christmas pageant. It was, David's outfit, the youngest of the five uncles, that Tucker needed. Down the middle of the family treasures was a safe path. Tucker maneuvered Bobby across the attic floor to the back steps that led right into Tucker's closet and bedroom. Halfway down the steep attic stairway, Tucker stopped.

"Bobby, sit right here on the steps. I'll have to get to my room the normal way, back out the window so I can walk in the door."

Tucker retraced his path: back up the steps, through the attic, out the window, down the antenna, across the limb, and out on the tree. When he came around the house to the side door, he brushed his sleeves and took a deep breath.

"Joseph," he heard Gramma say, "you want to check the back door. I feel a breeze."

"I'll check it for you, Gramma," Tucker offered as he came in the house. *It's closed,* he thought to himself, remembering the window. *I know it is.*

Tucker walked into the kitchen past the Frigidaire and down to the summer kitchen. The back door wasn't open. He knew the cold draft came when they opened the attic window. Luckily, he also saw the stack of evening newspapers Grandpop started to save for the next Boy Scout paper drive. Sure, the war was over, no more metal drives or old tire collections. But the Scouts still raised a little money for the newspapers. When he was in the fifth grade, he also helped with the milkweed pods drive. The military used the silk threads inside the milkweed to make parachutes. It was impossible to get authentic silk during the war. The Boy Scouts still got a little money for the newspapers they turned in.

Tucker found the newspaper from a few days before, brought it up into the house, and spread it out on the dining room table. Turning to the financial section, he ran his finger down the list of stocks and smiled. Yep, the price of a share of RTS stock had gone up. The previous paper proved it. Math had gotten fun.

"Tucker," Sam brought his grip up from the summer kitchen and placed it on the table. "Looks like you're pleased with your stock report."

"I am," Tucker remembered Betsy's accusation of lying and said no more about Wall Street's activities. If the rest of the family didn't believe him, he'd enjoy keeping his stock information close to his vest, or so the businessmen said. Tucker had no vest.

"Your grandmother said I could show you my pistols. Just don't touch them." Sam opened his small suitcase and took them out. "I thought if you had a chance to see them, you'd stop thinking about them."

Sam took off the holster and laid it with the pistols. The metal on the guns was shiny, with handles of rosewood. They reminded Tucker of the sidearms men of the old west carried. Rattlesnakes that slithered on the ground were often nearby, as well as the kind of snake that sneaks around on two legs. Those who lived on the frontier needed protection from both types of reptiles.

Tucker scrunched down as close to the pistols as he could without getting gun oil on his nose. His eyes twinkled like he had found a leprechaun in the corner of the garden. "They are amazing." Tucker's fingers twitched and itched to touch the weapons. He could see no reason why he couldn't just pick them up. The guns had no bullets in them. "I sure did wonder if I could make them twirl around like the cowboys in the movies."

Tucker closed his eyes and imagined himself standing in the dusty street of a frontier town in the Old West. The desperado facing him squinted in the noonday sun. Sheriff Tucker McBride's honest outweighed the gunman's experience. Tucker pulled the guns from their holster, twirled them around, and fired a shot before the outlaw could clear the leather. Marshall McBride shot the man in his boot. The gunman got on his horse and fled the town.

Sam broke into his fantasy. "I imagine you could twirl a pistol with the best of them. If you couldn't, I'm sure you'd teach yourself." Sam put the pistols in the holster. "Isn't it great that your grandmother has given you a chance to prove you're a man?"

Tucker's shoulders drooped. "What ya mean, Sam? I can't even touch the guns."

"Oh, I'm not talking about learning how to handle a gun. No sirree." He folded the holster carefully to put it away. "I'm talking about something far more important. I'm talking about an exercise in keeping your word. You told your grandma you wouldn't touch the guns, and I know you're a man of your word."

Tucker smiled to himself. That did feel better than twirling a pistol in his hand.

Sam yawned and rubbed his eyes. "Well, I'm tired. It's been a long day, and it started in the middle of the night under the big tulip tree in your backyard." Sam touched the pistols. "Your grandma said I could sleep the night in Joseph's big Morris chair. It reclines, and I should be just fine." He put the holster in his grip. "I see Joseph went to bed, so I'll take over his chair."

"I'm going to bed, too," Tucker mumbled as he slowly walked toward the stairs. He heard his grandmother call after him, "Another school day tomorrow. Get a good night's sleep."

Tucker suddenly remembered Bobby and stepped up his pace. He left him sitting on the attic steps in the dark. When Tucker got to his room, he closed the door and checked on his brother on the treads going up to the attic storage room. Bobby wasn't there.

Tucker's room was small. There was no place for another kid to hide. Then he thought of the one place that might work. It was the only place Bobby wouldn't be accordion-pleated all night. After his day stuffed in the Model A, Tucker was sure Bobby wouldn't want that contortion act all night. Tucker looked under the bed. There, among a few dirty socks, a lost baseball, and an assortment of crumpled papers, Bobby lay asleep, with Tucker's top blanket wrapped around him.

Tucker watched his brother sleep for a minute. *Should I wake him up or let him sleep?*

Bobby fit comfortably between the bare springs of the bed and the hardwood floor. His folded hands under his head provided a cushion while he slept.

Tucker could see no reason to wake him. So, he dropped his jeans to the floor and carefully slipped into bed so any squeak would not awaken Bobby. *It's kinda like the girls' slumber parties.* Tucker laughed to himself. *I don't think I'll use that term with the other guys, though.*

Chapter Ten
Smuggled Out, Not In

Morning broke like an insult, forcing Tucker's dreams to vanish. If a fellow could write his own dream script, creating the most entertaining movie-like images, it would be Tucker McBride. If awakened at night during a good dream, he went back to sleep and willed himself to continue the story. That morning was different. Bobby still lay asleep under his bed. Now what?

He checked the clock. It was 6:25 AM. He turned off the alarm and hung over the side of his twin bed. A quick exploration of the dust and junk under the bed resulted in Tucker's stomach-turning a somersault. Bobby was gone.

Tucker fought with the bedding wrapped around his ankles, kicked off the covers, and leaped out of bed. As Tucker grabbed his levies, Bobby darted in quietly and slipped around the door.

"Bobby?" Tucker gasped. "Where'd you go?"

"I had to go to the bathroom." Bobby started to giggle as he grabbed his mouth to muffle the sound. "I found it downstairs. When I came back up, the steps squeaked. Someone with a deep voice called out to you, or rather me. 'Tucker? You're up with the roosters.'"

Tucker rolled his eyes and whispered, "Grandpop." He pulled his T-shirt over his head and snapped up his long-sleeve flannel shirt from the floor. With his socks on and his clodhoppers* laced up, he straightened and stared. "What do I do with you now? I can't take you through the kitchen."

Bobby snapped his fingers. "Can I stay here in your room?"

"Won't work." Tucker looked around the room. "I'll go down and eat breakfast. You sit on the attic steps in case someone looks in the room, and I'll bring you some food." They agreed to the plan with a firm nod. Before anyone could come looking for him, Tucker slipped out of his room and bounded down the steps.

He knew Betsy wouldn't be up until the last minute. That was okay. She'd be in such a whirl she probably wouldn't notice any changes.

"Morning, Gramma." Tucker reached into the kitchen cabinet for a small mixing bowl and filled it with Wheaties. The familiar box with the picture of baseball player Hank Greenberg on the back was still half-full. "I'll get a few more boxes of cereal this weekend, Gramma." When his grandmother turned her back to pour her coffee, Tucker wrapped two large pieces of cornbread from last night's supper in a tea towel and shoved it under his plaid shirt.

"Halloween's today. Are you going out for Beggars' Night?" Gramma asked with a skeptical sound in her voice. "You seem a little old for Trick-or-Treating."

After positioning the cornbread, Tucker rebuttoned his shirt. "Christy wants to go. We'll walk down and pick up Freddie. Suppose we'll stay right here in the neighborhood."

Gramma looked up and glanced over her small glasses. "Make sure you're in by ten, Tucker. Late at night on Halloween is when mischief happens."

He gulped down the last of his cereal. Pouring some hot water from the tea kettle into the bowl, he added a few drops of dishwashing soap and washed it. Rinsing the bowl, he poured more hot water into it. Then he dried the bowl before replacing it in the cabinet. Tucker asked casually. "Gramma, where's Grandpop?"

"He was here a minute ago," Gramma said as she sipped her coffee. "Now, your granddad is sweeping off the sidewalk. It's late in the fall, but there are still some leaves coming down. Tonight, he doesn't want any of the children to slip on wet leaves when they come begging."

"I'll go up and get my books." Tucker wiggled around, trying to block his grandmother's view of the hidden food.

Gramma reached up into the cabinet. Stretching, she felt around to the back and retrieved a can of popping corn. She set the tin on the counter. "After school, I'd like some help making popcorn balls to give out to the ghosties and ghoulies tonight." Gramma checked on Grandpop out the window. She always tried to keep an eye on her nearly ninety-year-old husband.

"Sure, Gramma. If Christy comes over early, can she help too?" Tucker thought about how much fun it would be to get Bobby involved, as well. He wasn't sure how he could do that.

"Ya, Tucker. Christy would be a big help. She's a good girl."

Tucker ran back upstairs with more gentle steps. Usually, he would have shouted the whole way to the second floor for Betsy to get up. It made no matter that her alarm would go off in another ten minutes. It had more to do with annoying his sister than waking her up on time. This time he took the steps carefully, sidestepping the squeak on the fifth tread. He'd keep Betsy from crossing paths with Bobby for as long as possible. Betsy was smart with a keen eye. She might recognize who he was.

"Okay, Bobby. I have an idea." Tucker whispered as he opened the closet door and turned to gather his books. "Here's some cornbread. I'll get you out of the house while Gramma is in the kitchen and Grandpop is outside. I have to go to school."

"What am I supposed to do all day?" Bobby took a bite of the yummy, yellow bread. "Wow, this is good."

"Get your jacket. You're going to school with me today. Might as well see what Indiana schools look like." Tucker started for the hall door.

"Thought we'd have to go back out the attic window." Bobby watched as Tucker seemed to change the plans. He slipped his arm in one sleeve of his jacket and followed Tucker out the door, placing his feet in Tucker's footprints, like a skilled Apache tracking a bear.

Tucker stood for a minute and listened. Betsy wasn't stirring yet. The way his sister slept until the last minute, he didn't expect her to be awake. Tuck motioned for Bobby to follow him down the steps. In the front hall, he gave a hand signal for Bobby to go outside. Tucker opened the door, and his brother slipped out onto the front porch.

The fall morning was crisp. A lingering frost lay on the ground. Cramer's dog, Rosko, a block down the highway, was out for his morning bark to his female friend next door to the Cramer house. In the twilight before dawn, Bobby pulled his jacket tightly around him.

"Bobby, do you have any money?"

"Some. Why?"

"Right down there," Tucker pointed north where Moyer Avenue continued across the highway. "There, on the left, there's a little restaurant called the Coffee Cup. They opened at 6 AM. You'll see the lights are on. Go in and get a cup of hot cocoa to go with your cornbread. That'll fill you up." He pointed east of the house. "The school is in the next block. It starts at 8:10. Do you have a watch?"

"Yep," Bobby checked it. "I know where the Coffee Cup is. I found it yesterday at lunch. They serve a pretty good hamburger."

"So, it was you who got off the bus yesterday." Tucker seemed to put together another piece of the puzzle that was his life. "I thought the kid looked familiar. Now I know why."

"It was me, but I didn't see you."

"I was inside the station. I saw you through the window. Then, you were gone."

Bobby laughed. "I'm a Halloween spook. And, this ghost will see you at the school at 8:10," he repeated.

"Walk along the side of the highway," Tucker warned him. "Meet me there at about five 'til eight. Maybe I can bring a wig."

Bobby buttoned up his jacket and pulled his cap low. "How can I go into the school? Can just anyone walk in and say they're a student?"

Tucker rubbed his chin. "I have some ideas. Just meet me there, and I'll work out the details in the meantime."

"Okay." Bobby shrugged and started walking across the street.

Tucker watched him go. He had wanted to see Bobby for over a year, and there he was. Bobby crossed the road and hurried off in the direction of the Coffee Cup. "Details," Tucker mumbled as he closed the door.

"What ya looking at?" Gramma came into the living room just as the front door closed.

"Just some details," Tucker said with a crooked smile. "Just details."

Chapter Eleven
A New Kid in School

Tucker jammed the package he retrieved from the attic under his coat, hurried past his grandmother, and headed on out the door. Halloween morning was glorious, just the kind of autumn day that thrilled him and caused his heart to pump faster. He loved the nip in the air and the way the sun cast long streams of light across the lawn. The little bit of lingering frost made it perfect.

The last of the fall leaves laid in colorful piles along the fence row. Tucker knew Uncle Jacob and Grandpop would be out later with leaf rakes and the wheelbarrow to gather them. His grandfather would use the foliage as a layer to blanket the strawberry plants in the garden for the coming winter.

Where is he? Earlier that morning, Tucker arranged for Bobby to meet him in the bend of the alley. There was a deep sigh of relief when Tucker saw Bobby step out of the thicket of honeysuckle bushes, blackberry bramble, and wild-growing sugar maple trees. *"There you are."* But he worried inside. *What if someone saw him before I fix him up? Maybe someone remembers the family when they still lived in the area. What if a school friend of Bobby's mother came riding down the alley?* In Tucker's world, anything could happen that could interfere with his day of fun.

Bobby searched anxiously up and down the alley. "Tucker, you said you'd get here long before your school starts. I was worried."

"I brought something." Tucker pulled a crinkled paper sack out from under his coat. "Here," he said, chuckling, as he plopped a black wig on Bobby's head. "Uncle David and my mother used to portray Mary and Joseph in a Christmas pageant at church. I put Mom's wig on my head this morning before you got up, then plopped a mixing bowl on top. I trimmed it around the bottom of the bowl. That makes a good Amish haircut."

"Amish? What's an Amish haircut?" Bobby adjusted the wig until he seemed satisfied with its fit.

"The Amish people who live in this area like things very plain. They're religious but very old-fashioned, too. They don't even drive cars. They hitch up a horse to a buggy or wagon and go to town. The girls don't get their hair cut, and the boys have theirs chopped off at ear-length."

"Oh, okay," Bobby still looked confused, but he turned after he adjusted the wig. "How does this look?"

"Good." Tucker reached in his jeans pocket and pulled out a short red pencil. "I brought one more thing, Carolyn's eyebrow pencil. She has dark hair, so she uses a black pencil. You can't have black hair and blond eyebrows."

"Makeup?" Bobby drew back. "I'm not wearing a girl's eye makeup."

"Ya gotta, buddy."

"No one at your school knows me."

"Betsy does, and Carolyn will track you down and figure it out if she suspects." Tucker paused with the eyebrow pencil poised to darken Bobby's brows.

Bobby hung his head. "All I wanted was to spend a normal day with you. That doesn't seem too much to ask."

"Won't your mom be scared?" Tucker thought of his grandparents as he darkened his brother's eyebrows. "One day, some friends and I decided to hop on the train and go into Goshen. We ended up miles away. That was a day to remember. When we got home, the whole house sparkled with lights. Gramma was so worried everyone came over to sit with her and welcome us back."

Bobby shrugged. "I'll call Mom later today. By the time she gets here, Halloween will be over."

"There." Tucker stood back and admired his work as if he had just painted a masterpiece.

"Will they believe an eleven-year-old is an eighth-grader?"

Tucker shoved the eyebrow pencil back in his pocket and turned toward the school. "Some guys are tall, and others are short. Some are extra-wide, and others are as skinny as a broom handle. They'll believe it. They believe anything they think is on your permanent record. We'll tell them you just moved in, and your records should come soon." They stepped up their pace as they neared the side road in front of the school.

"Where will I be while you're in class?" Bobby stopped as they got near the school. "I don't want a teacher asking me a bunch of questions."

"I know you're wearing a disguise, but maybe you'd feel better if you were hiding someplace. There's a janitor's closet in the hall, down from Mrs. Hunter's room. You can spend some time there. If the custodian happens to come in, tell him you are in the closet to get a broom for Mrs. Hunter. You can climb a ladder in the closet that leads to the roof. Sit up there and enjoy the day. Or, the auditorium is in the same hallway, in the opposite direction of Mrs. Hunter's room. Go in there and take a nap in the back row. When you got up at six at my house, it would have been only 3 AM in California."

Bobby yawned. "You don't have to remind me." He yawned again. "What about lunch? Will the cafeteria serve me lunch?"

"I walk home at noon every day. You can come home with me." Tucker hurried into the school with Bobby at his side. As they stepped onto the tiled floor of the building,

Tucker lowered his voice. "With the wig, nobody should recognize you, here in school or at home. We'll find something for you to eat—peanut butter if nothing else."

"I like peanut butter." Bobby looked around the school and smiled. "My school building in Los Angeles is a lot bigger than this."

"Do you know all the kids in your school?" Tucker asked as he waved when his friend, Gilbert, walked down the hall.

"No. Just the ones in my class."

"Well, if you meet any kids here, you're going to have a friendly day."

Chapter Twelve
My Name is Norman

The school was teeming with ghosts, goblins, and ghouls. It was Halloween, and no one could do a costume party like the elementary school teachers. The enthusiasm spilled over into the middle and high schools. But the younger kids were the most excited. They came to school in fancy costumes, homemade, exotic creations, and colorful masks.

The day went unexpectedly well. When the bell rang for the lunch hour, Tucker hurried out into the hall to look for Bobby. To his surprise, his brother was down the hall helping the janitor. With a broom in his hand, Bobby was happily chasing fuzz and fallen papers down the hallway. A red shop rag hung out of his hip pocket. Tucker guessed the rag was to have available for a hidden cobweb or some spilled mystery substance. The lemony smell of Murphy's wood oil still hung in the air.

"Thanks, Norm," Tucker heard the custodian tell Bobby as his brother handed the broom handle over to Mr. Weaver. "You were a great help. Things got done a whole lot faster with you helping. And your company was nice for a change, too."

"Thanks." Bobby then offered to help Mr. Weaver even later. "I can help you again this afternoon during my study hall."

Tucker stopped in mid-step. "Norm … you have a study hall this afternoon? I guess I didn't know your schedule."

Bobby grinned as he pushed Tucker toward the door. "I was in the supply closet when the janitor came in. He said, 'Oh hi. You must be my helper for this morning.' I told him, 'Sure. I'm B…' then I thought and changed it to Norman. Norman Morrison lives next door to us in LA. He graduates this year. I didn't think the name would be familiar here."

"Sounds right to me, Norman." Tucker chuckled and led the way out the side door facing the alley.

"Tucker, wait up." Christy walked fast and skipped a little as she hurried to catch up. "Hi, Bobby. What's with the wig?"

"Does it look fake?" Tucker studied Bobby up and down and focused on the wig. "I trimmed a wig that was in the attic. Is it okay?"

Christy looked at Bobby again. "Wow, you were in school this morning?"

Bobby shrugged. "I was in the school building, not the classes."

Christy skipped a little to match the boys' stride. "It's good to see you, Bobby. I was going to ask my mom if she knew your mother. Then, I remembered I'd better not talk about it. You don't want anyone to know you're here."

Bobby's mouth popped open. "Thank goodness you didn't say anything. I don't want anyone to know where I am until after the fun tonight."

"No one?"

"Not until later today. I'll call Mom this evening." Bobby put up his hand. "Let's not talk about it anymore."

"Can't anyway. I promised. A promise is a promise, and you can't break a promise." Christy waved as she turned right and walked toward her home. "I'll see you guys back at school after lunch. Hope Mom fixes grilled cheese sandwiches."

Tucker and Bobby turned into the Moyer yard. Grandpop was raking in the garden just as Tucker knew he would. He didn't look up but acknowledged Tucker as he worked. "Hi, Tucker."

"Hi, Grandpop." Tucker put his index finger to his lips and kept going. He and Bobby walked right past his grandfather, and he didn't even hear him.

The boys slipped in through the summer kitchen and up the steps. Gramma was working with the meat grinder in the kitchen while another lady worked along beside her. Gramma was getting tired and had trouble with the metal, hand-crank, screwed-down grinding apparatus. She struggled to push the cooked meat into the opening at the top. She didn't look up from her work. "I'm up to my elbows in ground meat, Tucker."

"Mrs. Washington?" Tucker greeted as he passed her. "I didn't know you were going to be here. Glad to see you."

"Hi there, Tucker." Goldie used the back of her hand to brush a few strands of hair out of her eyes. "Good to see your smiling face."

"Ja, Goldie is helping with the mincemeat I make each year. She's learning how to make it so she can teach the ladies in her congregation in town how to put up a batch of jars. They're looking for a new money-making project. They can sell the jars at their Christmas bazaar. Our church does. Many families use mincemeat around the Christmas holidays."

Tucker looked through the dining room into the living room to see if Goldie's son was there. "Sounds good. Mrs. Washington, is Johnny here? I haven't seen him since last summer. Johnny was with us when we went to Goshen and ended up miles from there."

Goldie stopped for a minute and wiped her hands on her apron. "I'll never forget that, Tucker. Your grandma and I were worried sick. But I'm glad Johnny had the adventure." Goldie smiled a little. "Nina, my friend from church, is going to drop Johnny off here on her way to her sister's house for the weekend. Nina works in Elkhart and is going to

Indianapolis. It will be an easy stop for her to bring Johnny to your house. She's a good friend."

"Goldie and I will finish canning today and then label the jars after supper tonight. She and Johnny will stay for supper. Johnny would like to go out, Trick or Treating, with you this evening. While you boys are out, Goldie and I will put our feet up, drink a cup of cocoa, and relax while you children walk around town."

"That's great." Tucker motioned for Bobby to turn away a little to hide his face. "I brought a new kid home for lunch, B— Norman."

"Ja, gut." Gramma pointed to the big bowl of cooked ground-up roast beef. "There's the meat for the mincemeat in that pot. You boys can each make a roast beef sandwich. Enjoy a generous amount without being greedy. The mincemeat is for Christmas baking. Remember, a lot of us will make sandwiches. I want to put up several quarts of mincemeat and have them in the fruit cellar waiting for the holidays." She stopped and smiled. "The beef was at such a good price I might buy some more and can it, too. When I don't want to get out to the grocery, beef and noodles would taste pretty good."

"Sure, Gramma." Tucker motioned to Bobby to follow him to the pie safe where Gramma stored the bread. The whole cupboard smelled delicious, like yeast oozing out of every crevice in the wood. With two thick slices in their hands, they added the meat. On top, they heaped tomato catsup, mayonnaise, and Gramma's sweet sliced pickles. Just as they sat down at the table with their glasses of milk and sandwiches, Gramma brought up the topic Tucker didn't want to discuss.

"Your dad, Sean, called this morning," she started as she kept adding meat to the grinder and turning the crank. Lean chunks of beef pushed through the grinder blades producing strings and small meat chunks that fell into the bowl.

"Oh?" Tucker stuffed his mouth with a huge bite. "Wha- he wan-?" He knew Gramma would have a hard time understanding him. That was his plan.

"Tucker, you're talking with your mouth full," Gramma reminded him. "Don't take such big bites."

"Sorry, Gramma," Tucker swallowed hard and drank some milk to chase it down. "You said something just as I took a bite."

Gramma ignored his excuse. "He said, Bobby and his mother came to visit her sister, and now Bobby's missing." Around and around, she turned the crank, continuing to grind the browned beef. "Bobby left a note, but they're still worried."

"A note?" Tucker washed down another mouth full with a big gulp of milk. "What did it say? Where did he go?"

Bobby ate his sandwich and said nothing. He worked on his food but kept his eyes on everything beyond the windows, away from the conversation.

"Tucker," Sam Treadway came into the dining room. "Who's your friend?"

Tucker thought fast. "Norman Mc…McFarland. Today is his first day at our school. Thought I'd bring him home rather than fight through the cafeteria line."

"Welcome, cowboy," Sam offered his hand.

"Howdy, partner." Bobby wiped his hand on his jeans and shook Sam's hand.

"I didn't know Bobby was coming to Indiana?" Tucker said without looking at Bobby. "Dad didn't tell me. What did the note say, Gramma?" Tucker had to sound interested. He talked about wanting to see Bobby again for months. It would have seemed strange for him to show no interest in news about Bobby now.

Gramma stopped for a minute and stepped into the dining room. She looked at Bobby and blinked but then when on. "Your dad told me the note said something about wanting to spend the day enjoying Indiana, and no one should worry. With his wife and new baby, Sean said he really couldn't drive around town looking for him. Sean said, when his ex-wife, Bobby's mother, called him, she was worried. I cannot imagine how scared I'd be if you or your sisters were missing. It's hard enough wondering if Tim is okay and how he's doing in the Marines."

"If that boy isn't hurt or kidnapped, it sounds like he's okay." Bobby picked up his sandwich and held it to his mouth, blocking full view of his face. "Maybe he's just enjoying his freedom," Bobby offered as a possibility.

"Who are you, again?" Gramma asked as she squinted at Bobby.

"Norman McFarland," Bobby spoke up but held his milk glass up to his mouth, blocking part of his face.

"Mincemeat pie? That sounds good." Tucker tried to break Gramma's focus on Bobby. "How many quarts did you say you'll be able to make? And it takes, what, a quart of mincemeat for each pie?"

"You look familiar." Gramma started to walk closer.

She turned back toward the kitchen. "Well, I planned on six quarts for here at the house. Goldie can take home a couple of jars with her. Then the ladies at our church will get together next week and make the huge batch for the Christmas Bazaar. But if I don't get back to work, our pies here at home aren't going to be full."

After his grandmother got safely back in the kitchen, away from Bobby, away from all the questions about Norman she might ask, Tucker thought it was safe to ask about supper. "Gramma," he called from a safe distance. "Can Norm come back for dinner? His parents are busy unpacking all their boxes. His mom might not have time to fix supper."

"Ja, sure, Tucker. We're having hamburger stroganoff. There should be plenty. Give me his number, and I'll call his mother and tell her it's okay."

"The phone isn't connected yet, Mrs. Moyer," Bobby burst out.

Tucker popped up. "Norm can call her from the school office."

Gramma stopped and looked back into the dining room. "I thought he has no phone yet."

Tucker took a deep breath. "Oh, that's right." He thought fast. "A boy who lives next door to him can go over to his house and give his mom the word."

"Who is that?" Gramma asked from the kitchen.

"Can't think of his name right now, but I'll remember when we get to school." It suddenly dawned on Tucker how much he had been keeping the truth from his grandparents. *You have to tell a lot of lies to keep your word. There's a better way than that.*

Chapter Thirteen
The Smells Set Them Free

Back at school that afternoon, the teachers' scrapped their lesson plans for the last class of the day, no math, no English. Miss Skidmore, the gym teacher, led the elementary children through the school. In and out, the Halloween parade snaked from room to room as they displayed their creative costumes.

Tucker especially liked the outfit Pastor Dailey's son, Samson, had on. True to his name, he wore oversized, long underwear stuffed with newspapers where muscles would someday be. He carried a sawed-off black broomstick with black balloons tied to each end, simulating a five-hundred-pound barbell.

Clever. Again, Tucker's mind wandered off on a more creative topic than parading elementary children. *I'll bet I could be a weightlifter. Maybe I could go to the Olympics.*

"Class!" Mrs. Hunter tried to get the students' attention after the last clown left the room. "I realize Beggars' Night starts in a few hours, but I have an assignment for you."

Tucker slouched low in his desk chair. *Why do we always have homework on a super, great weekend?*

"Mrs. Hunter," Anna Frederick moaned in her usual poor-me style. "My momma has a family party planned for this weekend."

"Thank you, Anna." Mrs. Hunter smiled sweetly. "I hope you and your family have fun."

Gilbert spoke up quickly. "Birdie Kline's Sunday School is having an apple bobbing contest in the church parking lot tonight."

"That should be fun," Miss Hunter said with a smile. "Pastor Daily announced the apple bobbing contest during this morning's devotions over the PA."

Oh, right, Tucker remembered and thought of his brother. *Bobby would like to bob for apples.*

"Tucker," Mrs. Hunter gave Tucker an attend-to-me look. "Our history assignment is to interview someone. You're to say to that person, 'Tell me a Halloween tale from today or your past.'"

Anna grabbed her nose and gagged. "What is that stench?"

"Stench?" Tucker sniffed. "Smells good to me," he said. "It seems like the upper-classmen have put Limburger cheese on the radiators. They did it last Halloween, too. I happen to like Limburger cheese."

Christy laughed and shook her head in disbelief. "You like something that smells so bad you can't get it in your mouth because you can't get it past your nose?"

"It only smells bad if you don't like the cheese." Tucker laughed, sat back, and inhaled deeply with a broad, satisfied smile.

At that moment, the room PA squawked as the principal's voice filled the room. "It seems Trick or Treat has begun early. We will track down the Limburger cheese found on the radiator in the main hallway. We'll find the one, or ones, who purchased it. Not too many families buy a five-pound brick of cheese. We will identify you. Today, we'll have to close the school for fumigation. Luckily for us and bad for cheese spreaders, it's already Friday afternoon. Have an enjoyable Beggars' Night."

When the bell rang, Tucker couldn't wait to get out of the classroom. Bobby was either still pushing a broom or sitting on the school's roof, watching a gym class play baseball. Tucker jumped up, set on finding where Bobby spent the most exciting fall day of the season.

Chapter Fourteen
Treats

Tucker looked around for his brother, then saw him patting Mr. Weaver on the shoulder. "Hey, Bobby," yelled Tucker.

Bob pushed a wide broom around the floors, scattered with school papers and pieces of candy wrappers from Halloween parties some classes enjoyed. It was an early end for the school day.

"Bobby?" Mr. Weaver stopped abruptly and leaned on his broom.

"Sorry, Norm." Tucker rubbed his hand across his mouth, not to cover an embarrassing mistake but to stifle a laugh. "Don't know why I keep using the wrong name. I guess you remind me of my brother." He wrapped his arm around Bobby's shoulder and started pulling him toward the door. "Sorry, Mr. Weaver, gotta get home." They nearly jogged to the door. "What did Mr. Weaver have you doing?"

Bobby pushed the strange black wig back a little. His head was down, checking the floors so much the fake hair slipped forward. "We painted the stage door a bright red. The door is metal, so that was fun and exciting to learn how to do it. I like working with my hands." He turned his nose to the air. "But with the stink of that cheese, I am very ready to get out of here."

"That's good. Let's—" Tucker was jarred off balance and stumbled into Bobby as Vinny Wagoner, Gary's older brother, pushed past him. Gary was a good guy. As a favor, he drove Tucker and Christy out into the country one-day last year. He didn't have to. It was out of his way. Vinny would push you around rather than take you anywhere.

Vinny jostled Anna Frederick on his aggressive rush to leave the building. "We'll get a few guys and push that old outhouse over in one good, easy shove." Vinny pushed Anna again and kept on walking.

Tucker hurried to catch up to the upper-classmen. "You're pushing what over, besides us?"

"Keep your voice down, kid." Vinny got into Tucker's face with a sneer. "After dark, we're going out to the sticks and shove over ol' Harvey Wallheiser's outhouse." Then he grabbed Tucker by the coat collar. "Don't tell anyone."

"Right," Tucker agreed, but inside he thought, *who do you think you are?* "Come on, Bobby." He and his brother pushed past Vinny and his two dull-eyed cronies. They burst through the double doors and marched out into the late afternoon sun.

"Tucker," Christy called out as she jogged to catch up. "Are you guys going out Trick or Treating?"

"Don't know for sure. Gramma says I'm a little old for Beggars' Night."

Bobby wrinkled his eyebrows. "Beggars' Night?"

"Right, Bobby." Christy skipped along to keep up. "That's what we call it around here … and at my grandma's house in Ohio."

"Yep," Tucker said with a big grin as they crossed the street. "If I go out, Gramma wants me to stay in the neighborhood. She says I'm too old to go into other communities. She says I'd look greedy."

Farther up, where the alley made a bend, Freddie had already passed Moyer's gate. "You guys are slow. Don't you know it's Friday?"

"Bobby was helping Mr. Weaver. We'll let you know when we finish eating. If you want to walk around the neighborhood and collect candy, be ready later, when you finish at home."

Christy turned to go to her house. "Give me a call, Tucker. I'll walk around with you."

Tucker and Bobby went through the backyard and up into the kitchen. The house was abuzz with activity. Gramma was cleaning up all the beef that flew around from the grinder. Tiny helped clean the floor with each lick and bite. Sam popped corn, and Sarah was stirring something in a pan on the stove. Maneuvering through the small kitchen with Bobby, Tucker had Joe at his heels.

"Okay," Sarah said with a job-well-done tone in her voice. "I put in all the ingredients. I added: sugar, syrup, butter, salt, water, all of it. The temperature on the thermometer has reached what's needed, and I'm ready to add the vanilla. Then, that's it."

Tucker studied every task. It was easy to see what Gramma was doing. "Why popcorn on a Friday?"

Popping corn and cooking up some tapioca was Tucker's job on Sunday evenings. He usually made a double batch of both to last through the great Sunday evening radio programs the family enjoyed. Today, the pan on the stove was a mystery.

Sam checked a thermometer hanging from the side of the pan, removed the concoction from the gas burner, then placed the saucepan on a hot pad. "Quick. You two boys go in and wash your hands real good."

"Why?" Tucker asked but hurried toward the bathroom under the steps, just off the kitchen. Joe followed like a shadow of the boy. Tiny, however, seemed determined to stay near any food that might fall to the floor.

Sam didn't bother to answer the why question. "Hurry."

Heading toward the bathroom, Tucker saw Grandpop in his Morris chair, his feet up, listening to WOWO on the floor model radio with the push-buttons in the center for changing stations. "Hi, Grandpop," he announced.

Voices on the radio sang, "In a little red barn, on a farm down in Indiana." Grandpop answered without even opening his eyes, "Hi, Tucker."

The boys scrubbed their hands thoroughly with lava soap and hot water. Before leaving the small bathroom, Bobby pointed and asked, "What's that thing?"

"That's a razor strop. Grandpop runs his straight razor back and forth across it to sharpen it." Tucker picked it up and demonstrated the technique. "Then he pulls a single hair from his head." Tucker plucked out a strand from the top of his head, "and slices it in half with the razor from top to bottom." Again, he split the hair just like his grandfather. It was easy to see he had practiced often, whether Grandpop knew it or not. "Then, he takes this shaving brush," he picked up the short brush with an ivory handle, "gets it wet, and swirls it around on the soap in the shaving mug." Tucker demonstrated on a patch of face skin about the size of a postage stamp. "I tried to shave once, and my whole face turned red as if I'd taken off the first layer of skin."

"I don't think I'll try," Bobby decided. "My step-dad uses a safety razor."

Tucker opened the medicine cabinet and took out a silver-toned safety razor. "Grandpop does too. But he likes to use the old straight razor."

They came back into the kitchen just as Sam finished drizzling a thin line of the syrup Sarah made over the popped corn in a large enamel dishpan. Bobby's eyes danced. "You're making popcorn balls. I saw a family making them in a movie once."

Sam quickly tossed the corn and syrup together, lightly glazing all of it. "Okay, guys, dig in. Form as many balls as you can, and put them on the wax paper. We'll wrap them individually when they're all cool and shaped."

Carolyn darted in from school and sat down at the piano without taking off her coat and hat. She was short, just like Gramma, only four foot ten and a half. Carolyn would place her hands on the keyboard on the black keys, the sharps, and flats. She couldn't reach them from the white keys. She couldn't read music, but she could play almost anything she heard. She only had to listen to a melody once, and she could play it by memory.

"Gotta play this while it's fresh in my mind," she explained as she hurriedly played it. She played with both hands until the song emerged. "I have to go to work in a few minutes. Dalia wants to take her daughter Trick or Treating, so I agreed to work this afternoon and tonight. I answer phones until ten. The girls at school want to form a quartet and sing *The Old Lamp-Lighter* at the school talent show. How does it sound?"

"Wonderful," Goldie stopped for a minute and listened. "The old lamp-lighter from long, long ago," she sang along.

"Carolyn, you'd better hurry along," Gramma cautioned her. "You don't want to be late."

Carolyn stashed her books on top of the old upright piano and hurried to the door. "I'll have to do my homework late tonight. I'll work for Dalia again tomorrow. Won't have time then." She jerked the side door open and found a young boy standing there. "Oh, hi. Johnny," she greeted with a hug. "Good to see you. Gotta go."

"It's Johnny," Goldie gave a hearty laugh. "No one can let him in. We all have messy hands. We're either covered in beef broth or sugary syrup."

"Look who I found at the side door," Betsy announced as she shepherded Johnny Washington into the house.

"You're here." Tucker rolled another popcorn ball. "Wash your hands and dig in."

"Hi, everybody," Johnny said with a smile as he slipped into the bathroom.

With all the help, tennis ball-size treats soon lined the wax paper leaving the bowl empty. Sam snapped off medium size pieces of wax-coated paper, and the boys rolled up each popcorn ball, twisting the two ends to secure the closure.

"The trick or treaters will like these, I bet." Bobby's face, fixed in a permanent grin, positively shone.

Tucker put three popcorn balls back against the linoleum backsplash of the counter. "We'll get ours first before we leave the house."

"Ja. And put back one for Christy and one for Freddie, two." Gramma brushed some hair from her forehead and brought the broom and dustpan up from the summer kitchen. Her tightly twisted bun pinned to the back of her head slipped and came loose.

"Okay, guys," Tucker elbowed Bobby in the arm. "Let's wash the sticky off." He started again for the washroom. "Gramma, I'll help you clean up all this."

"Danke, Tucker. But I have many helpers and a small kitchen." She checked the red clock that hung on the wall above the sink. "We'll eat supper a little early, about 5 o'clock. That way, you'll finish in time to go to the Sunday school gathering and then visit some of the aunts and uncles for candy. You have about an hour." She emptied the dustpan into the trash. "And, take Joe with you."

"Yes, Gramma." Tucker petted the top of Joe's head. Tiny wedged her body between Joe and Tucker, prancing in circles. "I know you're here, Tiny. And, no, you can't go, too."

"Joe's a good dog." Johnny stooped down and shook the dog's paw, one gentleman to another.

"Wow, Tucker, two dogs." Bobby put his hand down for the dogs to sniff and get to know him.

"Yep," Tucker laughed, "two dogs and another brother. Life is great."

Chapter Fifteen
There Was a Crooked House

"Come on, Joe." Tucker put his coat back on and started for the door. "This one was a War dog." He reached down and scratched Joe's head. "He earned some metals during the fighting."

Bobby scratched the big dog behind his ears. "I thought those dogs never came home again. I read that somewhere."

"Most didn't." Tucker and Bobby bounced down the porch steps. "Uncle Jacob called someone or pulled in some favors or something." Tucker could see Bobby liked the dog. But then, who wouldn't love a dog?

Bobby followed Tucker and hurried along the sidewalk that led out to Moyer Avenue. "What are we going to do now?" Bobby asked.

"I have an idea. Come on." Tucker ran up to the corner, looked both ways, then darted across the highway. Mr. Winkler was gathering some mail out of the box near the road. "Hi, Mr. Winkler. Sorry, I can't help you."

"Didn't think you could help today. It's Beggars' Night." Simon Winkler said as he stood on the front drive of the little grocery store. He pulled his white apron up and wrapped it around his arms. "It's getting cold out here this afternoon."

Tucker waved. "I'll come over tomorrow and sweep your drive before it gets busy here."

Bobby shook his head, amazed. "You know everybody."

Tucker looked at Bobby in disbelief. "It's called a neighborhood, Bob."

"I know. I know," Bobby cracked. "I've seen neighborhoods in Disney movies. I just didn't know they really existed."

"Hey, guys, where are ya going?" Christy jogged over to the boys as they walked next door to Butch Randolf's Sinclair station.

"Well … I have an idea," Tucker said mysteriously. He rubbed Joe's head again to assure him they were a team and kept walking.

Christy stopped in mid-stride and put her hands on her hips. "What idea, Tuck? I've been on your spur-of-the-moment adventure trips before. Right, Johnny?" With a scowl still on her face, she turned to Bobby and forced a smile. "Hi, Bobby. Sorry. Tucker and I have had many adventures." She looked behind the boys. "Ah, yes … Mr. Cooper," she said with a grin as Freddie peddled up to them on his dad's penny-farthing, high-wheel bicycle*.

Bobby's eyes popped. "Holy Moly, Freddie. What are you riding? Where'd you get that thing?"

Freddie slid off the seat down the backside of the bike. The high-wheeler had a thirty-eight-inch wheel in the front and a small one on the back. "It's not the tallest one they made. Dad has a bigger one in the garage. First, it was my grandfather's. He was only about five-foot-ten. He wanted to be able to ride it safely, so he got a short one. When Granddad figured he'd ridden it long enough, he gave it to my dad. Dad lets me ride it once in a while if I don't let Tucker ride it."

Christy didn't even look at Tucker. "Smart man."

"Wait a minute." Tucker kept talking as he looked both ways before crossing the railroad tracks. "What did I ever do to your pop's boneshaker?"

"Boneshaker?" Bobby stared at the bike. "Why call it a boneshaker?"

"If you ever rode one, Bobby," Christy said with a laugh, "you'd know why. It isn't what you'd call a smooth ride."

"You did nothing to my dad's bike, Tucker." Freddie walked the bike across the tracks while holding on to the handlebars. "Because you never got to ride it."

"Bobby," Christy put her hand on his shoulder, ready to tell the next Tucker-tale. "Our friend Tucker rode Freddie's cousin's blue 1937 Indian motorcycle once. When he zipped out on County Road 13 on that Chief, he got it up to eighty-five miles per hour."

"Eight-five?" Bobby nearly choked on his words. "Holy Moly."

"Christopher Columbus," Freddie gasped, just remembering the motorbike ride. "I was glad my dad didn't see him on that thing." Freddie's expression twisted. "I guess he heard about it though. I think every farmer on County Road 13 saw Tucker whiz by."

"Again, let me repeat." Christy stopped where she stood. "I will not go to where you're headed before I find out where we're going. So, Tucker," she spoke with a teacher-like authority, "where are we going?"

"I'd like that information, too." Johnny started walking a little slower. "I prefer to know what trouble I'm going to get into before I get into it."

"We're almost there." Tucker tried to smooth over the plan.

Johnny, Freddie, and Christy all chimed in together. "Almost where?" Johnny added. "The last time you said we were almost there, we ended up in another state."

"I heard Vinny Wagoner and those two clowns he hangs with, Morty and Gus." Tucker's voice sounded sheepish but determined. "They were talking about going out after dark and pushing over Harvey Wallheiser's outhouse."

"Nice," Christy's mouth curved down in disgust. "Gary Wagoner's older brother?" Christy's voice raised at the end in a double surprise. "Wait, Tucker McBride. What does Gary's stupid stunt of pushing over an outhouse have to do with us?"

Tucker opened his mouth. "I thought—"

Christy put her foot down and turned. "I'm out of here."

"Okay," Tucker called after her as she stomped away. "But you'll miss the great stories everybody will talk about tomorrow." Then he remembered and asked, "Are you still going Trick or Treating later?"

"Sure." With her head down, she stomped away and kept moving.

Bobby watched Christy stuff her hands in her pockets. "What's an outhouse?"

Tucker couldn't believe the question. "You're kidding, right?" When he saw the blank expression on Bobby's face, he explained, "An outhouse is a tiny building or shack where the toilet is. Remember the old one in our backyard? They dig a hole in the ground and clean it out when it's full."

Bobby nearly gagged. "Pee yew." Then he thought again, "After his outhouse is lying flat on the ground, where will the guy do his business?"

"Harvey just put indoor plumbing in their house last year. He only uses the outhouse when he's out working in the fields and has mud on his shoes. He doesn't want to track dirt in the house."

Bobby shook his head in disbelief. "Then, that makes it okay?"

Tucker shrugged. "It's just fun, something to do. We can come back next week and set it back up for him. Besides, Vinnie was going to knock it down anyway."

"True," Freddie agreed.

They came upon the Wallheiser farm fast. I was just a half-mile east of the highway. A cluster of fruit trees was on the left of the house. The late afternoon sun was bright, sending flashes of light through the branches. The air was crisp. It was just the right sort of day to have another adventure. To Tucker's thinking, there couldn't be a better day for outside activity.

Freddie leaned the high wheeler against a fence post. The boys slipped into the yard beyond the apple orchard. Tucker hoped the Wallheisers couldn't see them as they approached the outhouse between the orchard and the barnyard. Tucker used hand gestures to direct his troops and motioned for Joe to stay silent as the dog waited for his work orders.

Tucker and the boys reached up, placing their hands on the west side of the small structure. The old, weathered wood was rough and full of splinters. Joe pranced back and forth. As they began to push, there was a loud *squeak* and a *crack*.

When they looked up, Harvey's BB-gun still straddled his folded arms. He had a long piece of straw in his mouth that bobbled when he spoke. "That was fun, I bet ya." The old farmer squinted from where he took his stand on the other side of the barnyard. "Now, you boys run along home."

"Thanks." Tucker waved as he backed off, smiling his usual broad grin. He knew, with Mr. Wallheiser's aging eyesight, he probably couldn't actually see who had attacked his outhouse, so Tucker saw no need to give him a verbal source of recognition.

"I heard the BB-gun." Bobby looked back at the outhouse. "But what was the cracking sound?"

Tucker looked back again. "I do believe it was the building. Doesn't it look like the outhouse is leaning?"

Chapter Sixteen
An Uncle Jacob Story

Grandpop had finished the evening grace when Gramma passed the noodles. "Tucker, just about a cup for each of ya. If there's more, you boys can have seconds." Next, she passed the ground beef gravy topping to complete the helping of hamburger stroganoff. To Tucker's nose, it was an aroma only a crack-shot chuckwagon cook could create, hitting the bullseye every time. It smelled like browned meat and onion in just the right portions to tickle anyone's taste buds.

Goldie watched as they passed the serving bowls. A slight frown crossed her face. "Rebecca, are you sure you have enough for Johnny and me? I don't want you to be short."

"There's enough, Goldie. I'm sure. I even got out a freshly baked loaf of bread and some peanut butter for anyone who is still hungry." Gramma passed the plate of thick-sliced bread. It still smelled yeasty, was soft to the touch with a crunchy crust. "There's plenty to eat."

"I'll have some of your great bread, Mrs. Moyer." Johnny smiled with a twinkle. "That way, I won't take as many noodles."

"Help yourself to both, Johnny," Grandpop assured him. "God always seems to provide enough when unexpected company is present. There'll be plenty." He spooned a generous amount of Gramma's jelly on top of his buttered bread.

Gramma pointed to the round mound of butter on the small old plate on which her mother served churned spread. "When the government rationed everything during the War," she told the guests, "I made all the family's butter. Uncle Jacob drove me out into the country to buy milk. I'd pour about half the cream off the top, but not all of it. Pa doesn't like *blue milk,* he says. Then I'd churn the cream into butter."

"That's amazing, Rebecca," Goldie marveled. "I have never churned butter."

Gramma unfolded her napkin. "I was blessed. I still had the old butter churn Mama used."

Betsy served herself some stroganoff but didn't take her eyes off the boy who called himself Norman. She looked at him with a studied eye. "What did you say your last name is, Norm? You look so familiar."

Bobby, startled by Betsy's digging into his identity, nearly choked on a mouthful of bread. "Norman McFarland," he coughed and cleared his throat. Then he stuffed his mouth full of stroganoff. "Not from around here." His last words were hard to understand, but that's what he wanted. "Just moved in."

"Do you have an older sister or brother in the high school?" Betsy moved closer into Bobby's space.

"Back up, Betsy," Sam cautioned as the girl stretched across the table in front of him. "I'll be dropping your grandmother's great homemade noodles in your hair."

"Yew," Betsy moaned and scratched the top of her head.

Bobby looked from Johnny to his mother. "Where's your dad? Is he coming out later?"

"He died in the war," Johnny said as he looked out the window that faced Moyer Avenue.

"That's what mom said happened to my dad." Bobby picked up his glass of milk and looked into the white creaminess. His set jaw revealed his growing anger over the lie. "But it wasn't true."

Johnny stirred the meaty gravy into the noodles. "People never heard much about black G.I.'s who served in the war, not even the ones who were heroes." He looked at his mother, smiling a little with pride. "Dad was in the final push into Germany toward the end of the fighting. A sniper's bullet hit him when his unit came into Merkers-Kieselbach, Germany. The Merkers Mine is where they found all that Nazi gold."

"Oh, wow," Bobby whispered and looked down at his plate. "I'm sorry."

Tucker quickly changed the subject. "Enough of that sad stuff. Our class has an assignment for Halloween weekend. We're supposed to gather a family story about a memorable Halloween from the past. To me, they've all been fun. The story doesn't have to be my experience." He looked around the table. "Any of you have a good one to share?"

"Well," Cousin Sarah appeared to search the ceiling for a unique tale. "Nope, can't think of any. We lived in the country. We didn't walk along narrow, dirt roads on Halloween. We celebrated at the end of October at our church by having a big harvest party."

"Besides," Sam added with a chuckle. "You could step in some horse stuff that would destroy the aroma of freshly made popcorn balls and wonderful chocolate cupcakes."

Grandpop put down his coffee cup and sat back. "I have no Halloween stories. I started working on the railroad when I was ten years old, carrying water to the men. On scorching hot days, I'd have to run back and forth what seemed like a hundred times a day. That was about 1872. Booth killed President Lincoln just seven years before that. There was no time for play or parties, except for family and church time at Easter, Thanksgiving, and Christmas."

Sam stuck his fork in his food. "Times were different then, Tucker. Kids walked out of their innocent years and jumped into adulthood with both feet. I remember many things from a few years back." He closed his eyes and seemed to see pictures in his head. "If I start talking about the past, I won't stop for days. I can talk about the wind whistling through the mouth of the caves of Carlsbad Caverns in New Mexico, and the October 31, my friend Charlie López and I started into the cavernous space. It sounded like ghostly spirits had flown out and danced a jig on the ground outside. Then, there was the time Cargo Willy and I decided to take a steamboat down the Mississippi River in 1927. We had heard about the flood and wanted to see if there was anything we could do to help. By May of 1927, the Mississippi River south of Memphis, Tennessee, was sixty miles wide. We were in the area until Halloween."

The family just looked at him, wondering if his tales were tall or true. Gramma saw their expressions of doubt and jumped in. "You sent that necklace to me from New Mexico. Someone made it out of obsidian they found on the desert floor. It was beautiful."

"Right," Sam closed his eyes again and smiled. "The Apache tear necklace." He put down his fork. "Kids, an Apache tear, or obsidian, is black volcanic glass, formed at a time many, many years ago, when an old volcano erupted, and the lava rolled down the mountainside, tumbling some of the lava into round pieces of glass called obsidian. The native people called them Apache tears."

Bobby stared at him for a minute. "Is that true?"

"Of course, it is," Uncle Jacob answered quietly. "I read about those semi-precious stones in the National Geographic.

"I've seen Grandma's necklace," Betsy testified. "She let me wear it one time to a party."

"I have a story for you," Uncle Jacob took the bowl of green beans Gramma passed and dished out several spoonsful.

"Oh, ja?" Gramma seemed surprised Jacob was offering a Halloween story. "You usually like to read in the evening, not go begging."

Sam sat up straighter. "I'd like to hear this one, Jacob."

"There was one special Halloween in 1914." Uncle Jacob scooped up another forkful of stroganoff. His story-telling was slow to begin and very detailed once started.

Tucker put down his fork, placed his elbows on the table, and listened intently. He loved to hear a good family story. "How old were you then, Uncle Jacob?"

"I was about fourteen years old. Dad had come home from his week away, working on the railroad." He smiled and gestured to Grandpop. "But he had a lot to catch up on. Mother sent me out to the back-forty to bring in the cows. It was near milking time. I remember Halloween was a Saturday that year. I had gotten up early that morning since Dad got home the night before. I looked forward to spending some time with him."

While those at the table sat motionless, waiting for the events to unfold, Jacob sipped coffee from his cup. He took his time with everything, not from being slow of mind but from a need to include every tiny detail. Jacob would meander around the story like the Snake River. Tucker thought Uncle Jacob was the only man alive who could come to the dinner table after the dinner bell rang by going out through the summer kitchen to put the rake in the shed he forgot about earlier and come back through the side porch entrance while everyone waited for him at the table.

Jacob continued with a sheepish smile. "I was pretty sleepy, and I wanted to stay awake to help Mother pass out cookies to the neighborhood ghosts and goblins. Since the cows were in the lower pasture, I took my fishing pole along to see if I could get any bites. It was warm that late October. Some summer grasses were still standing in the ditches that bordered the fields. When I put my fishing line in the water, I took off my shoes and laid back on the grass to get more comfortable. Now that sounds reasonable, doesn't it?" He put a bite of noodles in his mouth. "It wasn't long until the warm sun and Indian Summer air caused me to fall asleep."

Again, he stopped and ate some more food. Tucker and the others quickly saw it would be one of Jacob's long stories and continued eating while they listened. It was like eating popcorn on Sunday night while *The Adventures of Sam Spade* filled the living room with suspense.

"When I didn't come back by milking time, mother sent Uncle James and a couple of his friends that were hanging around that day out to get me. Finding me asleep, Jimmy hurried back to Dad's workshop and got a can he saw earlier. I was so tired from waiting up for Dad the night before that I was sound asleep. When I woke up, I found that Jimmy had painted my feet green. I was so mad, I pulled on my shoes and quickly found them full of the same paint. I stomped and sloshed every step of the way back to the house. Since it wasn't water-based paint, Mother wouldn't let me inside until the paint dried so I could peel off the green stuff. I sat out on the porch 'til after dark until I finally got it all. Dad put my shoes in the trash pile. They were old, but they were my favorite everyday pair." He sipped some coffee. "I don't think I got over being mad for a couple of weeks."

Everyone at the table burst into laughter. As Uncle Jacob looked around, a small smile began to spread across his face until he broke out in laughter, too.

Betsy always liked good Uncle Jacob stories. "No, Uncle Jacob. I don't think you got over being mad until now."

"Maybe you're right." Jacob dug into his dinner, but the smile didn't fade.

Tucker gave Bobby a little elbow jab. "That will make a good story for my homework." Then, his eyes brightened even more as Gramma began passing out pieces of apple pie.

"Now, Tucker…you boys can have a second piece when you get back from apple bobbing. The time is near."

Tucker studied the slab of golden, flakey crust hiding a mound of sliced, sweetened apples for only a few seconds. Then he dug in. The minute his fork broke through the crust, the delicious aroma of cinnamon was set free. "Umm, good pie Gramma."

Bobby sat amazed. "Holy moly, you have a snazzy family."

"Yep, I sure do." Tucker agreed. "Snazzy."

Chapter Seventeen
Basement Treasure

Everyone gathered their plates and cups from the table and took them into the kitchen. "Why do I always have to help with the dishes, Gramma," Betsy whined as she put the milk glasses on the counter beside the sink. "Tucker gets to go over to the church for the apple bobbing contest. He never has to help." She took the dishes Johnny handed her and stacked them neatly with the plates she had already placed there.

"Well, now, Betsy," Sarah patted the fifteen-year-old on her shoulder. "I'm here. I'll help your grandmother with clean-up. You can go over to the church if you want to. That is," she added quickly, "if it's okay with your grandma."

Sam came up close behind Sarah. "I can dry dishes. I worked for my grub in San Francisco some years back by washing and drying dishes. During that trip, a bank robber made his getaway by running through the *High Mile Eatery* kitchen and shot me in the leg. Infection set in. The doc had to cut it out."

Gramma came up from the summer kitchen with the two dishpans she stored under the dry sink. Taking the large tea kettle from the back burner of the stove, she filled the pans. Then she pumped in water from the pitcher pump to cool it down enough to put her hands into it. "You wrote me about that one, Sam. With all the dangerous experiences you found yourself in, it's a wonder you're still alive."

"Thank you, Sarah." Betsy shot back through the kitchen door as she grabbed her coat and dashed outside.

"Going to Stuart's house. Nancy and I will spend the evening together," she added.

"Have fun," Gramma called back. "Be home by ten."

Tucker looked out the window. "The street light came on, Gramma. It's time to go over to the church parking lot for apple bobbing." Tucker pulled his coat from the hall tree by the side door and tossed Bobby his. Sam's white Stetson hat and a black mask made up the rest of his costume. "Sam said I could borrow it for a few hours. I'll go out tonight as the Lone Ranger."

"What is apple bobbing?" Bobby quickly shoved his arms into his jacket sleeves as he hopped down the porch steps.

"Just wait," Tucker said as he jogged across Moyer Avenue with Bobby and Johnny close beside him. "Birdie Kline, our Sunday school teacher, always organizes the contest every Halloween. At least for as long as I can remember." Over at the church, Tucker joined the few who had gathered already.

"Johnny Washington. Good to see you. Hey, Tucker, who's your other friend?" Yvonne Sherbet asked. She wore a crazy green and orange, large-check clown costume, and a curly orange wig.

"Norman McFarland. He's almost a cousin."

"Almost?" Yvonne wrinkled her forehead. "How can someone almost be a cousin. They either are a cousin, or they   aren't."

Tucker had to think fast. With his grandparents just across the street, they could find out about Bobby. And Bobby wanted no one to find him. If he told anyone at the apple bobbing contest, the secret could get back to Gramma, and that would end their special day. "Norm is a new kid around here."

Gilbert looked at Bobby carefully. "Yeah, you're cousins. You kinda look alike." He smiled when he turned and saw Johnny. "Hi, John. I haven't seen you since you visited our Sunday school class months ago."

Christy had on a colonial dress, complete with a white apron and dust bonnet. "What did you guys do before supper when I went home? Did you shinny up a flag pole or walk on a tight rope across the Elkhart River?"

"Nope." Tucker's statement was short. Flag poles and rivers were not involved.

"Johnny! Good to see you." Brandon Frederick, Anna's cousin, walked up and gave Johnny a proud Boy Scout salute. "When does this thing start? I want candy."

"We still need to set up some bobbing stations," Birdie Kline announced to the few who had arrived early. "Be patient, and we'll begin soon."

"Come on," Tucker motioned for his friends to follow. He walked up the four steps that led into the main hall of the church. He turned back to Mrs. Kline, but she wasn't watching.

"Tucker McBride?" Christy whispered as she passed some parents who were helping set up the event. "What are you doing?" Some of Tucker's antics were fun, some were a little dangerous, and some could get them all in trouble.

"The church is open, and Grandpop and Gramma aren't around. There are a few nooks and crannies in there that I've never seen."

"Like where?" Freddie asked, with a surprised raise of his brows. "I thought you hadn't missed one square foot of floor tile in this place."

"There isn't any floor tile where I want to go." Tucker opened the door, and they all quickly slipped in. "I've been in the furnace room a lot." He kept walking until he came to the basement door. "I've helped Grandpop carry buckets of ashes up from the coal furnace since I was a little kid. He used the ashes to fill potholes in the parking lot."

"Okay?" Bobby slowly questioned as they came to the dimly lit area under the church sanctuary. "If you've been down here," he shivered a little and pulled his coat around him, "then what did you miss?" His eyes searched the darkened corners.

"So…you're not interested in exploring, Bob?" Tucker moved slowly toward an opening to another room.

"Not so you'd notice," Bobby said softly and stayed close to Tucker.

The basement was dry, not like some cellars that smell musty, like wet concrete soaked in gym socks. In the back rooms, there were more spider webs the deeper back they moved. Christy jerked and pulled away from every hanging something, just in case it might be an occupied web.

"Look what I found," Johnny said when he reached for a black knob that turned on a single bulb hanging from the ceiling. With a lowered voice, he announced, "Let there be light, and there was light."

The poured cement walls of the room looked painted or white-washed at one time. Over time, most of the white stuff peeled off and lay scattered on the floor. That made the room look even older than the pew-filled room above it, dingy and shabby. Church workers hadn't stored very much in the small room. It looked like someone had put a few things in the corner, closed the door, and forgot they were there. On the right was a pulpit chair, tall and carved with fancy scrollwork, adorned with a worn-out gold cushion on the seat. The wood was dusty and streaked with something sticky.

Christy asked, "Wonder why they didn't just recover the seat?"

Freddie looked at the chair and shrugged. "My dad says sometimes it's cheaper to get rid of the old and buy new."

Tucker ran his fingers over the finely carved wood frame. "My Gramma says, hanging on to the old things helps us remember where we've been and who helped us get here."

"Like in your attic," Johnny chimed in. "There is lots of old stuff up there."

Bobby pointed at something in the corner. "What's that?"

Tucker squinted in the dim light. "That looks like a tombstone." Slowly walking closer, he strained to see the lettering on the old piece. "It says something on it." He turned to Freddie. "Would ya find a rag and wipe that off?"

"Down here? That would be dirt cleaning off more dirt. Not me," he refused. "Let's try to figure it out from here." He lowered his head, "And I'm not Fraidy Freddie. My oldest cousin called me a Fraidy-cat. I wouldn't walk a tightrope he stretched across their big pigpen. Then he changed it to Fraidy Freddie. He sang that worn-out silly jingle all last summer."

Tucker scratched his head. "Have I ever called you that?"

"No," Freddie admitted. "Must have just been my sweet cousin. Okay," he said, dusting off his hands. "I'm done with that." He squinted toward the tombstone. "Let me see, Loving Wife—"

"Loving mother—" Christy added.

"Loving Fr…Friend." Bobby finished the epitaph. *

"Elizabeth…" Tucker took a few steps closer. "Elizabeth Naomi Yoder."

"Who was that?" Christy asked as she got close enough to read it easily. "There are Yoders among the Amish. I don't know any that live around here."

"Lived Christy, lived, not lives." Tucker pointed to the fading print below the name. "Born 1792, Died 1837."

"She was only forty-five years old," Christy whispered.

"Pioneer women worked hard," Tucker said as he ran his fingers over the dusty, wooden grave marker and thought of his mother. She also died young. The worn, carved wood raised splinters as he fingered the surface. "It's dry enough to turn to dust anytime now."

"What's the thing doing down here in the basement?" Bobby asked. "I didn't even see a cemetery around the church."

"There isn't any," Freddie whispered and stepped back a few steps. "I get spooked by cemeteries and things that belong there but aren't."

Tucker turned and started back toward the basement steps. "They had to move a portion of the cemetery at the Poplar Tree Church when they widened the road. They re-buried those bodies at Pleasant Grove. It looks like they misplaced one of the headstones. Hum, Elizabeth Naomi Yoder. That name sounds familiar. I'll ask Gramma. Some of her people were here for so long. There's a parchment deed hanging on our dining room wall, signed by President John Quincy Adams."

"Wow," Bobby marveled. "A president is hanging on your wall."

They started up the stairs and down the hall when they heard the chatter and laughter of Sunday school kids from the parking lot. The over-active, over-curious bunch pushed the door open boldly and joined the group outside. Tucker's curiosity was satisfied for the moment, but he knew it would require a more permanent gratification.

Chapter Eighteen
Apple Bobbing

"Okay, everyone." Birdie Kline stood on the church steps, then turned and paused for a second. "Johnny Washington. I didn't see you. Did you just get here? It's nice to see you. Is your mother here, too?"

Johnny did a pretend bow. "She and Mrs. Moyer are making mincemeat."

Mrs. Kline raised her hands. "I'm glad you're with us. I've known your mother for years. And, I'm sure the mincemeat will be wonderful."

Johnny waved a little. "Some of the kids on my block get a little too tricky on Trick or Treat night. I'm glad we came here to celebrate Beggars' Night."

"Then, this is the place to be." Birdie pointed to the materials she brought. "I brought two of my washtubs, borrowed two more, and filled them with water. So, choose up to four people per tub. Each member of the group will bob for apples. When it's your turn, sink your teeth deeply into that apple. Go far enough past the skin you can lift the fruit out of the water with no hands. Then it's the next person's turn to step up to the washtub. The first group to complete bobbing with all members securing their apple, that group wins. The prize is a coupon for each member to exchange for a soda or banana split at the South Side Soda Shop in Goshen."

The entire group of teens, smaller kids, and a few parents erupted in cheers and clapping. Everyone looked around and pointed out four friends. Tucker and his group quickly banded together to take on the apples floating in a tub nearest them.

"It won't be as easy as you think." Birdie pulled her hair back and wrapped a ribbon around it, forming a ponytail. "First, find a way to hold your hair back. You can't have your hand up to your face since you have to keep both hands behind your back. I tried to snap off all the apple stems, so don't think the stem will help you. You'll only contact the apple with your teeth. Now, go to your washtubs."

"There are five of us in our group." Tucker added, boasting. "But we'll still get done first."

Each group circled a large gray galvanized laundry tub filled three-fourth full of water, with apples floating on the top. "There are at least eight apples of various varieties in each tub. That way, if you get a small bite but the apple falls on the floor, you have a few more to chase around the water. You have to clear the side of the tub and hold it in your teeth. You can only use your hands to take it out of your mouth. Then you can go ahead and eat it. Enjoy the wonderful harvest of fresh apples."

Darla raised her hand and shook it frantically in the teacher's face. "Mrs. Kline, there are five in our group, too. No one wants to be the odd-man-out and go to a different tub."

"Okay, parents, I need three volunteers to help them out. One from Darla's group will—"

"Mrs. Kline, it isn't Darla's group," Anna complained. "The group doesn't belong to anyone."

"Of course not, Anna. Thank you." Birdie cleared her throat and started again. "If two of the group go to the last tub, we'll need one parent in this group." She pointed to the non-Darla group. "Then, we'll need two parents in the last, new group to complete the four."

Most of the mothers stepped back a few paces and shook their heads. Thelma Frederick whined, "I just washed my hair this morning." She sounded just like Anna. The class nicknamed Anna *Miss Woe* because she always complained. She'd moan with a sigh, "Woe is me."

Three of the dads stepped to a washtub. "Just call me Georgie." Darla's father, George Crabapple, joined Darla's group. "Besides, apple is in my name."

"Do you have to stick your head in the water?" Bobby watched as the first person in each group bent over and readied themselves for the "GO" signal.

"Well, yes." Tucker couldn't believe that Bobby was afraid to put his head under the water. "Didn't you say you went swimming with Jack Benny's grandchildren? If you can swim, you can hold your breath."

"Well, yes. I didn't think of that." Bobby continued to watch intently.

"Do you like apples?" Tucker wondered if Bobby's aversion to the dunking activity was a dislike for the catch, or bite, in the case of apple bobbing.

"Sure," Bobby looked squarely at Tucker. "I don't know anyone who doesn't like an apple."

"Everyone ready?" Mrs. Kline warned. "*Go!*"

Christy clapped, jumped up and down, quickly jerking the white cotton dust bonnet from her hair. All around the parking lot were sounds of laughter and cheering as other groups tried to capture their first juicy piece of fruit. Christy watched a small apple float around the water for a second, then dove her teeth down into the water, snatching the apple in one try. She laughed and quickly stepped out of the way. "That was the smallest apple in the tub."

Johnny stepped up in a snap, held his breath, and dunked his head in the tub. Instantly, he captured a small yellow apple and jerked it out.

"Good job," Christy said with a giggle in her voice. She grabbed one of the towels Mrs. Kline provided and handed it to Johnny. "Dry off, or drip dry, whichever you please."

Bobby started to rest his hands on the side of the washtub until Anna yelled, "Hands behind your back." The youngest McBride ignored the outburst but jammed his hands in his pockets. The first try at a large red delicious apple landed Bobby ears-deep in the water. Sputtering, he aimed for the apple again and liberated it from the tub." He was so excited he waved the apple in the air and did a victory dance. As Tucker prepared to dive in the tub, Bob continued his celebration of fun.

Mrs. Kline laughed and called out, "Go ahead and eat it, Norman."

Tucker had already singled out the apple he'd go after. The washtub was one of the round ones and not square like some. There was no corner to help trap the apple. Tucker clasped his hands behind his back and snapped at the apple. He felt like a seagull, darting down to surprise a fish that floated too close to the surface. In one strike, Tucker had the apple in his teeth. He stood victorious with his hands up in victory.

Freddie chased a Granny Smith apple around the washtub. He followed it up and down, then quickly bobbed for the apple that finished the group, catching it in his teeth. In all the dunking and bobbing, Freddie splashed water down his front and into his shoe. He sloshed on one foot as he pranced around the parking lot.

"They're going to hear us coming, Freddie boy." Tucker nearly doubled over with laughter. "You need to change your Halloween costume theme. Here comes the monster from the watery lagoon," he howled.

Tucker and Bobby dried their faces on one of the towels Birdie Kline brought from home. Tucker flipped the end of the terry cloth to Bobby, who used the other end. "We won!"

Freddie's chest puffed out. "And, I brought in the last apple." His smile, blocked by the large red delicious apple in his mouth, had the added accent of apple juice running from the corner.

"And the winner is ..." Mrs. Kline said while laughing at all the dripping faces around her, "tub number one, Tucker, Christy, Freddie, Johnny, and Norman. And here are your ice cream coupons."

Bobby's eyes danced as he twirled around the tub. "I've never had so much fun. Now what?"

Christy watched, shaking her head in disbelief. "Have you never celebrated Halloween before? What on earth did you and your friends do in California on Halloween?"

Bobby stopped his dance for a second and shrugged. "I don't know—stuff. Nothing very memorable."

"Yeah, yeah, we won, we won," the five chanted as they joined Bobby in his dance of victory, circling the tub.

"That's not fair," Anna said as she frowned. "They had five people in their group."

"Anna, five apple-bobbers take longer and make it harder to win, not easier," Mrs. Kline reminded her.

"Harrumph," Anna snorted, folded her arms, and stalked away.

"Good job, Tucker." Grandpop put his hand on his grandson's shoulder as he came up beside him. "You are the winner."

"Great, Tucker. You guys, too," Sam said with a laugh and a handshake. "Your team was fast and skilled. It reminded me of 1930 when I watched Notre Dame's Fighting Irish play over in South Bend. Knute Rockne's boys followed every team play to the letter and won. Just like you five. You developed a plan, and you worked the plan."

Grandpop spread his arms out. "Gut. Gather together, and we'll form a different team. With your help, Sam and I will have those junior choir risers out in no time."

"Risers, Mr. Moyer?" Freddie asked.

"They're stored in the big closet off the fellowship hall. We set them up when the junior choir has a special

Christmas or another holiday program." Visitors to the neighborhood can sit on them today to watch the Halloween parade."

"Halloween parade?" Bobby looked at Tucker. "What's that?

"The neighborhood kids, cousins, and friends from other neighborhoods, come over and have a parade of their costumes. It kicks off Trick or Treating." Tucker followed Grandpop and Sam into the church, with Bobby and friends close behind.

Down the hallway, they turned left into the gathering area. That's where the ladies of the church served large dinners, and the Youth Fellowship played shuffleboard. Large closets with wide doors that Grandpop made years ago lined the back wall. Grandpop took a key from his pocket and unlocked the space.

"I made a sled on wheels to carry the risers down the hall," Grandpop told the boys as he pulled out something that looked like a four-foot-long skate. "We'll have to do one set at a time."

"Okay, Grandpop, maybe you and Sam can use the sled. You can steer, and Sam can balance it. I think Bobby, Freddie, and I…" he paused and looked at Christy. "Christy, you can help us carry another set out by hand."

His grandfather smiled. "Tucker, that should work."

Each team had its set of risers. The four carefully lifted the metal frames, bent, and welded into a shape that looked like wide steps. Fourteen-inch wide, wooden planks laid across the frame, end to end, to create the treads or risers. With Grandpop and Sam on the skate mover and Tucker and his friends using only muscle, two trips brought out four sets, plus a small free-loader.

"Gut, gut. Thank you all. It would have taken me a long time by myself. Ma and I will sit on the side porch and watch all the cowboys and princesses go past. The rest of the people will enjoy the bleachers." Grandpop looked up into the dimming sky. "Looks like a beautiful night."

Tucker locked the storage room closet, then ran the key back to his grandfather. It was getting darker by the time Tucker came back. A few cars had started pulling into the church's parking lot behind the bleachers. "I brought something out for you, Christy," Tucker said with that unique tone that meant mischief was imminent. "I found this in the closet." He put his hand in his jacket pocket, and like Little Jack Horne, he pulled out a mouse. "What a good friend am I."

Bobby and Freddie jumped back. Tucker thought they screamed like the screech owl in the rafters of Noah Dominick's barn. "Oh, yikes!"

Christy rolled her eyes, an optical exercise she completed nearly every time she was with him. "Tucker," she oozed with a sugary voice, "you thought of me. Thank you."

She took the mouse by the tail, held it up close to her face, and appeared to inspect it. "Too little," she announced. "I reject you. You're defective." She paused, glared at Tucker as only Christy could, then threw her gray, icky, fuzzy present across the lot. It landed on the hood of Principal Metzger's Buick. Everyone recognized Metzger's car.

"Eek!" All the visitors in the church parking lot heard Mrs. Metzger yell. The mouse didn't bounce off the car and land in the grass at the side of the lot. It tangled its tail in the car's windshield wiper on the passenger side. The mouse spread out on its belly with its little beady eyes looking through the glass, staring at Mrs. Metzger.

"Woops." Christy moved over closer to Birdie Kline. Wanting to draw attention away from the rodent, she asked sweetly, "Can we help you carry the washtubs someplace?"

"Thank you, Christy." Mrs. Kline put the last half bushel of apples in the back of her Ford Woody.*

Dusk had faded to dark. Tucker tied his red bandana-style handkerchief around his neck like a cattle driver. "I have my Lone Ranger mask in my pocket."

Children in all styles of costumes began to gather at the head of the parade. Like almost everything in Dunlap, the head of the line was at the church.

Bobby stood back and shoved his hands in his pockets. "Those kids look kinda young."

"They are," Christy agreed.

Booby watched them walk past. "Out in California, young kids don't go out without their parents."

"We're a neighborhood," Tucker said with a soft smile. "We watch out for each other's kids. Gramma said to just go to a few houses, families, and people we know. I don't want to look like some big kid just out for loot." Tucker kicked a few stones off the blacktop in the parking lot. "We'd better go Trick or Treating. Gramma doesn't want me out too late. She says, only mischief happens after dark."

Christy took another big bite of her apple. "I'm allowed to stay out until ten."

"Good." Tucker started walking in the direction of Aunt Franny and Uncle James' house. "We'll go down to Tweety's."

"Tweety's?" Bobby closed one eye in confusion.

"That's another story," Tucker said with a laugh.

"Okay, Mr. Boy-of-Many-Stories, tell it," Christy commanded.

"Alright," Tucker gave in. "I was down at Aunt Franny and Uncle James' house one morning. My cousin Rosie was still in bed. Aunt Franny's bird was singing from the cage. Out in the kitchen, Uncle James got his own breakfast and sat at the table eating. Aunt Franny came in and found a box of canary food on the table. 'I just opened this box of food for the bird yesterday. Now it's empty.' She walked over to the table and inspected Uncle James' bowl. 'James,' she snapped at him, 'you're eating the canary food.'

Uncle James just kept on eating. So, now we call him Tweety."

Bobby laughed. "You have a family that would make a comedian wealthy."

"Do you think?" Tucker thought and laughed inside. "It's never quiet around here, that's for sure." As they walked south down Moyer Avenue, he added, "Later, we'll come back to my house and check out our stash of treats on the front porch. That should be okay with Gramma."

Tucker could see down to the end of the road. Aunt Franny had the yellow porch light lit. She used a yellow bulb to chase away moths to make front porch sitting more enjoyable. To Tucker, the light meant they had candy for neighborhood kids, or it indicated, the James Moyer family was still up.

To carry the candy loot he would acquire, Tucker had a medium-size, striped cotton bag Gramma made out of feed sack cotton material. Earlier in the day, he rummaged through her box of fabric bags. He selected three blue and white striped ones for Bobby, Johnny, and himself."

Gramma didn't let anything go to waste, even colorful cotton feed-sack cloth. When Grandpop emptied the hundred-pound sacks of chicken feed, Gramma would wash the material, separate the floral-patterned fabric sacks at the seam, and sew the yard goods into dresses. Carolyn and Betsy wore them when they were younger. From the less attractive feed sack cotton, she created draw-string bags. Some became totes for a special baked treat for friends. The family used others at Christmas in place of paper wrappings. Gramma never threw anything away.

Tucker pointed to the house. "Uncle James goes to bed early so he can get up before sunrise to go to work." Tucker was proud that his uncles continued to work through the Great Depression, then the world war. Now, they worked long hours of overtime to meet the needs of a growing population during the post-war years. "Saturdays are different. Sometimes he works extra hours, but usually, he doesn't work on the weekend. He needs to keep a regular schedule so he doesn't fall asleep in church."

"My step-dad works hard, too. Even my mom has a business." Bobby smiled broadly like he never thought about his family's work. "In Los Angeles, a lot of people work for the film industry. Mom makes baby layettes. Some of the movie stars buy them for their new babies. They are handmade with tiny details."

Tucker remembered Bobby talking about the fancy clothes for babies. "Right, a baby layette."

Bobby laughed. "Mom can make a lot more money when she calls the stuff a *layette* instead of baby shirts, nightgowns, and diapers."

"Yeah," Tucker thought for a minute. "How did we get into talk about baby nappies?"

"Baby diapers?" Christy giggled as she joined in the conversation. "I didn't even know you knew what a nappy is, Tucker."

"I know a lot of things." He thought for a minute, then he added, "Maybe sometimes the things I know aren't connected. I'm a master of information and an amateur at details."

Chapter Nineteen
A Snitch's Surprise

Tucker pulled the cloth, draw-string bag out of the hip pocket of his jeans. "We won the coupons for a soda or banana split at the South Side Soda Fountain. Mrs. Kline gave them to me. Here ya go." He passed one to Christy, Johnny, and one to Freddie. "Bobby, I'm going to stuff yours into the bottom of your sack." He put the fancy orange coupon into the blue and white striped bag. "Maybe Uncle Jacob can take us to Goshen tomorrow for our rewards. I want a huge banana split."

The late October evening was turning colder since the sun slipped farther over the western horizon. Streaks of crimson and coral still warmed a corner of the sky, but Tucker wondered about Bobby's warmth. *Wow,* he marveled to himself. *I have to think about a little brother.* "Bobby, are you warm enough?"

"I am hot," he sang out as he ran ahead down the road.

Christy watched and smiled. "I would say Bobby is having a good time."

"Bobby," Tucker called after him, "turn right." He verbally steered his brother like a side-riding stunt rider into the short driveway leading to his cousin Jenny's house. "Family lives here."

"Family? Great." Bobby darted into the drive and waited for the other four to catch up. "I've never seen so many family members in one area before."

The four walked to the door together while putting on their false faces. Suddenly, the door flew open as a tiny ghostie, with a white pillowcase pulled over the ghostly head and large holes cut out for eyes, stood in the opening. "Hi, Tucker." The apparition giggled and jumped up and down with excitement.

"Hi, Violet." He reached down and rubbed the top of the spook's head. "Are Etta and Zoey out Trick or Treating?"

"That big bully stole our candy," a blond, curly-headed, seven-year-old snapped. "Zoey and I ran home. They said they'd snatch us the next time. They'd put us in a big gunny sack and drag us home."

"Don't worry," Tucker soothed as he put his hand under Etta's chin. "We're around the neighborhood. "Do you know the bully's name?"

Etta wrinkled her brow. "Maybe. His brother is Gary Wagoner. I know, 'cause he used to be our paperboy."

"Vinny Wagoner..." Christy sighed with her lips in a perch.

Shirley, Tucker's cousin, brought out five large five-cent Hershey candy bars and dropped one in each sack. "Have you seen those kids that bothered the girls?"

"Not since school." Tucker's eyes brightened when he studied the candy bar. "Thanks for the chocolate." To Bobby and his friends, he added, "Let's run home for a minute."

They all gave their thanks and shot out of the drive. The Moyer home was back a few houses. Tucker led the way through the summer kitchen door, past the dry sink, and up the steps. The kitchen still smelled like a blend of onion, deeply browned meat, and the rich sour cream of the stroganoff.

"What are we doing?" Christy asked as she watched him open a kitchen cabinet.

"We're gonna get a bully," Johnny boasted.

"A candy thief is the worst kind." Tucker reached behind the saltbox, the container of cinnamon, and fished for something in the back.

Bobby stretched and tried to see what Tucker was doing. "What are you getting?"

Christy shook her head and rolled her eyes. "Sometimes, it's a good thing. Sometimes, it's not."

Freddie looked toward the dining room to see if anyone was close. "Like that time at school. He used the flag's pull chain to take a bucket of balloons to the top of the pole. Then, he shinnied up." Freddie whispered, "When two senior girls, all dressed up for a choir program they were supposed to be in later that morning, came out to raise the flag, he threw water-filled balloons down near them. He planned to startle them, not hit them."

Christy covered the side of her mouth. "Courtney Bixby just had her hair done at the Fancy Spot Beauty Shop the evening before. She looked so angry I thought she would return fire. It splashed right in front of her, but to Courtney, that was too close." Christy quickly grabbed her mouth and looked around to see who was watching when the others started snickering.

From the cabinet, Tucker removed a package sealed in a yellow wrapper with dark brownish-red trim. In the candy bag, he pulled out the candy bar his cousin just gave him. Carefully, Tucker opened the end without tearing the wrapper. He laid them side-by-side and studied their size and shape.

"Oh, I get it." Freddie nodded in agreement. "Good idea."

"What?" Christy and Bobby asked in unison.

"Watch," Freddie whispered.

"I think I saw Mrs. Moyer put it back there. Mom was shaving off a tiny bit of cheese into one of your grandmother's little bowls. Your uncle put some on his stroganoff."

"Johnny, you know too," Christy asked, then smiled.

Johnny reached in the drawer and fished around through the utensils. 'My mom uses something like this to decorate the top of chocolate cakes." From the back of a drawer, Johnny pulled out a cheese grater. "This what you were looking for?"

Tucker smiled, tore off a piece of wax paper, and smoothed it on the countertop. He removed a square of Gramma's unsweetened Baker's chocolate and carefully shaved off the top with the fine grating side of the cheese grater. That smoothed the piece down, similar to the thickness of his milk chocolate candy. He snapped off a square of his Hersey's bar, replaced it with the unsweetened reshaped bitter piece, and popped the yummy sweet chunk in his mouth. Carefully, he folded the wrapper around the bar, put his hand under the pump in the sink to dampen his finger, then touched a small spot so the paper would seal.

"There," Tucker announced as he picked up the one-of-a-kind candy bar. "Let's go back and see if Etta can help."

When they got back to his cousin's house again, Tucker was already feeling guilty. "I'm sorry, Shirley. Maybe I shouldn't ask."

"Ask what?" Shirley blinked and looked again at the group standing at her door, dressed in homemade Halloween costumes.

"We'd like to catch Vinny Wagoner, Shirley." Christy burst out.

"How?" Shirley looked down at Etta and Zoey, who had gathered around her legs. "I know someone should stop those kids. How can I help?"

"I have a special candy bar for Vinny." Tucker took the bar from his bag and held it up. "Give Etta a small grocery sack and put the candy bar in it. If Vinny grabs the bag, it won't matter if it's just an old paper one."

Bobby grinned and pounded proudly on Tucker's shoulder. "He fixed the bar by trading a piece of a Hersey for an unsweetened piece of baking chocolate. He won't even smell the difference. The sweet chocolate overwhelms the Bakers piece."

"Oh," Shirley rubbed her hands together, "that sounds delicious." Then her mouth curled under in a gag. "Well … actually, more bitter than yummy." She paused, then started to smile. "I love it."

With their masks back on, Etta carried the ammunition sack while Zoey had the empty one. The night was darker by that time, so the girls had flashlights. Their father, Ben, was a member of the volunteer fire department. He had many hand-carried lamps around the house. Ben sat in the dark area, away from the porch light, where he could keep his eye on his girls.

The last of the fall field crickets chirped in the darkness. Each loud chirp sounded like a marching beat as the group advanced on the Wagoner gang.

The beams from the flashlights cast a glow down the street, while Tucker and his friends lagged behind the little girls in the shadows, about twenty feet back. From behind a tree in George and Mary Fry's yard, three dark figures suddenly darted into the road. The taller figure jerked the loaded sack from Etta's hand, and one of the short goblins took the empty one from Zoey. Tucker and the four friends shot toward the girls and encircled them with their arms. No one was going to put them in a gunny sack. Tucker was sure of that.

"Thanks, girls." Christy, Tucker, and the others hustled Etta and Zoey back to their house. As they walked up the drive, they all heard a strange sound from a backyard down the way.

"Ugg," was the first shout they all heard. Then some favorite words respectable people don't use, to Tucker's way of thinking, came drifting through the night air.

Tucker's shoulders pulled up to his ears as he put his finger to his lips. They all listened again.

There were the disgusting sounds of gagging, spitting, and yelling. "Bitter chocolate! Who had that brilliant idea?"

Morty and Gus, the same pair who hang on Vinny every day, were the other petty thieves. As they emerged from the shadows, Tucker caught a glimpse of the trio as he and his friends darted into Shirley and Ben's living room.

"We got them!" Bobby threw his hands in the air. "Bitter chocolate for a very bitter guy."

Freddie checked out the front door. "Looks like they're gone."

"Finally," Tucker saluted Shirley and Ben. "Thanks, guys. That was fun." He looked again. He searched up and down the street and along the tree line behind the houses across the street. "Yep, they're gone." Finally, they all stepped back out into the night.

The treat or tricksters began to thin out as Tucker and friends walked down to where the road made a bend. They stopped at the house on the left. The yellow porch light was still casting a festive glow on the sidewalk. Aunt Franny, dressed in a floral print cotton house-dress and large floppy, gray sweater, came to the door. She carried a basket with a big orange bow tied at the top.

"Tucker, I was thinking of you when I bought these new, chocolate-covered coconut bars with a couple of almonds on top. They're called Almond Joy." She quickly spoke to the other four. "I have Heath Bars if you'd rather." Then she whispered to Tucker. "You can eat more than any child I know, Tucker. You can have a Heath Bar too, along with your Almond Joy."

"Thanks, Aunt Franny." Tucker opened his cloth tote and let his aunt drop the bars inside. He wondered if Tweety was home but thought he'd better not use the nickname the neighbor children and cousins called him.

Neighbors along the way gave all kinds of candy, most of them covered in chocolate. Babe Ruth, Snickers, and

Three Musketeers were some of the names of the delicious bars. They were all now available since the war was over. Jim and Joyce Dunlevy, around the corner, wrapped up salted peanuts, in half-cup portions, in squares cut from last Sunday's colorful Comic section of the newspaper, then tied the little pouches with string.

When the five got back to Tucker's house, they sat on the front porch and watched the night traffic go past on the two-lane highway out front. "Gramma," Tucker called when he opened the front door. "We're out here on the front porch."

"Ja gut," Gramma answered.

"Any candy to spare?" Grandpop called from his Morris chair in the living room.

"Grandpop," Tucker called out. "You're still up?"

"Ja, I bought a new crossword puzzle book today."

Tucker grabbed up his candy loot bag and stepped into the house. "Peanuts, chocolate-covered coconut bar? Does anything sound interesting?"

"No lemon drops?"

"No, but someone gave me a roll of Life Savors. How about that?" He reached in his bag and brought out the hard fruit-flavored candy with the hole in the middle.

"Ya. You're a gut boy." Grandpop reached for the multicolored roll of candy and smiled.

It was nearly nine o'clock when they got back to the porch. Tucker sat on one of the metal tulip-shaped chairs and threw one leg over the arm. The night air smelled clean and crisp. The owl that always returned to the willow tree in the front yard hooted its questions of the night - hoo, hoo, hooooooo. "I'd say we had a pretty good haul. Glad you were along, Bobby."

"Me too," Bobby agreed and reached in his bag for a piece of his loot.

"But the evening's not over," Tucker smiled with that smile that could bring fun or flop.

Chapter Twenty
Overheard in a Maze

"What did you have in mind, Tucker McBride?" Christy asked in her usual the-only-grownup-in-the-room tone.

"Christy, it's nothing prankish." Tucker smiled a mischievous smile. No one knew if the smile meant he was teasing or hiding the truth.

"Right . . .," she stretched out in disbelief, waiting to experience the outcome.

Tucker got up and started to step off the porch. "We'll take the car." He stepped back and pulled the front door open. "Gramma, we're going out for an hour."

"Ja, gut Tucker," she called from her sewing rocker in the living room.

"I know where we're going!" Christy squealed. "Frank Moody's corn maze." She started after Tucker and motioned for the boys to follow. "Come on; it's safe."

"Corn maze?" Bobby fell into step behind them. "What's a corn maze?"

"You don't have them in California?" Freddie questioned. His voice curled up at the end in disbelief. "What do they have in California?"

Bobby shrugged. "The Pacific Ocean and a lot of movie stars."

Freddie responded meekly, "Well, there is John Wayne."

The five of them started to pile into Tucker's car. "Do you want to ride up front, Christy?" Tucker asked.

Christy smiled and started toward the back. "I'll give Bobby that time with you." Joe nuzzled her leg as he walked by and sat down on the ground before her. "Do you want to take Joe? He can sit in the back, three in the front and three in the back."

Tucker threw his head back and laughed. "Sure, why not? It's only about two miles. I'll be comfortable. I'm in the driver's seat. You guys will have to bunch together."

What a load, packed in a small car! Tucker, Bobby, and Johnny sat in the front. Of course, the weight, not evenly distributed, listed toward the passenger door to give Tucker more room to drive. In the back rumble seat, Christy and Freddie squeezed into the soft, brown leather seat. Joe stretched across their laps. Tucker was pleased when the A Model moved under the heavy load. As the little black car started to cross the highway, Joe raised his head, sniffed the air, and let the wind rush through his soft black and tan hair.

Tucker checked Winkler's Grocery before passing the corner. He always thought of the front of the store as his responsibility. He also thought of the yeasty smell of Mrs. Custer's dinner rolls Simon sold on Saturdays. It was a habit. "We'll turn just past Dad's house, Bobby. Don't worry; he won't see you."

"I know," Bobby said. "But it feels like he will."

"I didn't know there was a corn maze out here," Johnny said. He strained in the dark to see the farmland that stretched for miles behind the houses facing the street.

"Frank puts a maze out every year." Tucker shifted slowly, then turned right at the corner. About a half-mile down on the left, he pulled into the field marked off for parking. "He makes good money on the maze each year."

After their children were all grown, the Moody family worked together to lay out the best five-acre maze in the area. With two sons and a daughter, they were able to plan and plow out an elaborate path in their cornfield, with blind alleys and lanes that went nowhere.

The field of corn stalks, saved after harvest time for the maze, stood over seven feet high in tightly planted rows. No one could see over, and no one could see through. There were two openings. The entrance was at the east end of the field facing the road, and the exit was sixty feet west.

The old Ford rumbled and bumped over the parking area, rutted by many other visitors. "Everyone out," Tucker announced, like a sergeant leading his troops. Joe got out first and stood ready.

"I don't have a flashlight," Christy admitted as she caught up to Tucker. "I wouldn't want to be lost out there in a dark maze and not be able to see anything. I don't even know my way out of things when the sun is at high noon."

Tucker was excited and quickly added, "I helped Frank order and pick up a couple of dozen flashlights for people who don't bring one."

"It looks amazing this year." Christy clapped her hands together. "We only need a couple of flashlights if we stay together."

"Do all of you have money?" Tucker reached in his jeans pocket and found some change. "It's fifty cents each for the four of us." He pointed to Christy, Freddie, and Johnny. "And, since Bobby isn't thirteen, he pays a quarter." He turned to his brother. "I have a quarter for you, Bobby."

"I have some money," Bobby insisted as he fished through his pants. He nearly turned his pocket inside-out when he pulled out a handful of change.

"Let me do it, Bobby," Tucker insisted. "Call it a lot of years of birthday presents."

"Tucker," Frank Moody reached out his hand for a hearty shake, "you brought friends for the flashlight walk."

"Right, and we all need a flashlight. None of us brought one. Well, I kinda brought Christy and the guys out here without telling them where we were going." Tucker looked into the opening of the maze and saw only dim shadows. The moon was out, but it was still dark in the maze.

"Okay, I just have two flashlights until a couple more people walk out of the corn." Mr. Moody handed over the beams. "If you decide not to stay together, make sure each group has one of the flashlights."

"Thanks, Frank." Tucker took one of the flashlights and handed the other one to Johnny. "We'll stick together. But, if we become separated, make sure you're with one of us." He looked around in the darkness. It was hard to see without a flashlight. Testing to see how far the beam would travel, he focused the light on the large bank barn* and chicken coup in the barnyard. Across the barn near the roof was ***John Yoder Farm - established in 1830.*** "This is where I saw the name. Frank, does your family know Elizabeth Naomi Yoder?"

Frank thought for a minute. "My mother's great-great grandmother's name was Elizabeth Yoder. She and her family settled on the Elkhart Prairie sometime around 1829. Elkhart County first placed its county seat right here in Dunlap in April of 1830. Later they moved the county seat to Goshen since it was closer to the center of the county."

"Well, Frank," Tucker paused for a surprise effect, "we found Elizabeth's headstone in the basement of the Dunlap Church."

"What?" Frank's mouth dropped. "We wondered where that grave-marker went. Tucker, I owe ya." He shook Tucker's hand with his right and patted the boy's back with the other.

Bobby threw his hand to his face. "Sounds like everybody owes you, Tucker."

"Nah. No one owes me anything," Tucker said with a sheepish grin. "I explore the neighborhood and find things. Then, I get them back to their rightful owner."

Each dropped their money in a padlocked coin box Frank had screwed down to a table and entered the maze.

"Hey, wait for me," Freddie called out. "Once you turn the corner, the night overtakes everything."

"Are you afraid of the dark? Doesn't the moon help light the way?" Christy asked.

"Sure," Freddie rubbed his arms like the coldness of the night penetrated his bones. "I just don't like the *dim*."

"I understand." Johnny flashed the light along the path in front of Freddie. "You're not afraid of the dark, but the dim seams spooky, like *The Mummy Stalks the Corn Maze*."

"That's it." Freddie moved to the lead position but still within the limits of the two beams. "This way."

Straw bales, stacked six bales high and eighteen inches deep, added additional form and sturdiness to the walls at the entrance and the exit to the maze. "Look," Christy said, pointing, "they left a few bales at the side of the pathway. A maze-walker could sit and rest if they got lost or tired." She started counting each bale from where she stood to where the path turned. "I wonder how many bales there are in the field along the corn path?

"Frank's equipment makes each bale forty inches long," Tucker offered. When everyone looked at him in surprise, he added, "I've helped him bale straw and detassel corn." Tucker held the flashlight under his chin, pretending to be a ghoul, and spoke with a ghostly accent. "If you *vant* to know how many bales *vere* used, count *zee* ones you pass, and add some extra for the false branches."

"Never mind." Christy turned and ignored the stacks of straw. "I'm not that interested anymore." She swished her full skirt and entered the maze.

They walked along the path of corn stocks and four straw bales. Then they came to the first right/left maze decision.

"Which way, Tucker?" Bobby asked. "You helped layout the maze, didn't you?"

Tucker pointed his flashlight right, then left. "I helped bale the straw, not cut out the maze." He studied the straw path under their feet in both directions. "Look at the straw on the ground. It looks like the kids that went ahead of us tried both directions."

"I can't see over the stalks." Christy stretched and craned her neck. Looking at the four other guys, she added, "I guess none of us can. It's going to be a guessing game all the way."

When a beam from another flashlight crossed their path, a mom and two young boys came around the corner. "Hi, is this the way out?"

"Sorry," Johnny gulped with a giggle. "This is the way in."

"Oh no," the boy missing his front teeth moaned. "I'm tired." He stomped his feet as he followed his mother.

"Let's go this way," Freddie suggested the opposite direction the mother and her children had chosen. "If they're lost, following them seems to be a bad choice."

"Freddie, my friend, I think you're right." Tucker looked both ways as he patted his dog on his head. "What do you think, Joe, which way?"

The dog's military training snapped into focus. The greying and tan German shepherd stood at alert, facing the left path.

Tucker aimed his beam to the left, and they all followed the light. "Good job, Boy." Tucker patted the dog's neck and pointed forward. Johnny brought up the back of the group with the second light.

"How long will this take?" Bobby looked down the dark path in both directions. Then the maze came to a dead-end, with branches stretching east and west. "It's clouding over. With no moon, it will be even darker."

At the next intersection, Tucker paused a brief second and turned right. "Most corn mazes of this size take forty-five minutes to an hour to complete."

Christy followed, staying close to Tucker's heels. "Don't forget Tucker's unbelievable sense of direction."

"Really?" Bobby straightened a little, as one would who just heard there was a way out of a hundred-acre jungle full of monkeys, lions, and other such scary animals.

"Well, now Christy, don't forget last summer," Johnny reminded.

"Right," Freddie added with a little stored-up shiver and a hint of doubt in his voice. "We started on a little six-mile trip and ended up one hundred thirty-five miles away."

"But we weren't lost," Tucker insisted with a laugh. "I didn't make one wrong turn, not even once."

Christy shook her head. "That's because railroad tracks don't make right and left turns."

At the next branch of the corn lane, Tucker turned and then turned again. Suddenly, he stopped, put his finger to his lips, and pointed to the path beyond the straw-lined wall.

Voices from the maze path beside them sounded impatient and angry. Joe's ears stood at alert. A voice graveled out, "It's time to re-decorate Wallheiser's outhouse for him. Let's get out of this crazy, people-size spiderweb."

Tucker looked at the dog and quickly put his first two fingers over Joe's mouth. Joe sat back on his haunches and looked to Tucker for directions for his next move.

Another voice snapped back from beyond the stand of corn. "How Vinny?"

A third, weaker voice chimed in. "When we find an opening, let's get out. I don't care if it's an entrance or an exit. It's still out."

"When we find one?" the first guy growled. "You dunce, we can make a door. These corn stalks are dry. We can set the whole field on fire."

Tucker nearly jumped to his feet. When a voice spoke out, he hunched down again.

"Vinny, there are kids in this maze," the other one bellowed out.

Tucker and the four heard the sound of straw bales falling to the ground, silly laughter, rough-house pushing, and the flip of a pocket lighter.

"Hey, you. Stop!"

Tucker strained to see through the corn, but it was too dense. Someone sounding like Frank came along to stop Vinny's rough nonsense. Tucker crouched lower in the lane, and the others followed his lead. Joe lay at alert on his belly, stiff and guarded. Tucker mouthed, *Vinny.*

He heard another snap of the lighter, and the smell of smoke and burning corn immediately filled the air. They all caught the sound of crackle, crackle.

Joe jumped up quickly, growling, with his ears laid back. Tucker jumped to his feet. "Pull um down," he whispered to the others.

The five jerked the heavy bales like they were boxes of feathers, clearing them away from the growing fire. They could not let the straw add more fuel to the flame. Each was surprised by their own strength. But how would they get to the other path to put out the flame?

"Who would do such a thing, Pop?" they heard another voice ask. "Who starts a bonfire with people in the middle of it?"

"Three rapscallions, trying the trick side of Trick or Treat," Frank growled. "But this trickster doesn't care who gets hurt."

Tucker heard the ting, ting of a fire extinguisher. When he realized that Frank came prepared for anything, Tucker smiled.

"They already started pulling this bale apart," one of the younger Moody men grumbled. "They tried to use it for tinder."

Tucker could smell the phosphate as Frank's son sprayed the foam over the fire.

"It's a good thing you decided to patrol the maze in the dark tonight," Frank said.

Then, there was the sound of huffing and puffing and the scrapping of straw rubbing together. It sounded like Vinny, and his two roughnecks, managed their getaway.

Tucker and his friends stayed low, but all nodded in agreement. They agreed it had to be Vinny and his two henchmen. They started walking, bent at the waist until they came to the next turn. "Okay, we're near the exit, and the three clowns should be gone."

A few more turns with Joe in the lead, and they saw the light at the end of the corn stalks. The dim lightbulb, placed low to the ground, didn't shine brightly enough to beam over the top of the corn or give a clue to the way out. Frank Moody's oldest son, Carl, had rigged up a neon exit sign he placed on an old, wooden child's chair. It sat at the final opening in the sweet-smelling wall.

Tucker and the others hurried toward the old Ford. Piling in, Tucker breathed a deep sigh. "I think the front porch will be the safest place to wait out the rest of Beggars' Night."

Chapter Twenty-One
Visitors from the Sludge

The tall clock in the entry hall chimed ten times. Christy stretched her legs, pumped the wooden porch swing a little, and rubbed her eyes. The chains that connected the swing to the porch roof squeaked with each movement to and fro. "We've been out here a long time. It's late. I'm cold. I'm going home."

"Yep," Tucker agreed. "Gramma said she wanted me in by ten. But we're going to walk you home first." He started to stand up. "I'll tell Gramma."

"I can walk her home," Freddie offered. "Her house is just past mine."

"Thanks, Freddie." Tucker pulled his jacket more tightly around him. "I feel responsible."

Christy put her hands on her hips and glared. "Well, I do thank you, Tucker McBride. But you're not saying I can't get home by myself, are you?"

"Of course not." Tucker stammered. He'd learned not to doubt Christmas Tree's strength and self-confidence. And, he had learned to call her Christy a long time ago, not what her mother named her. "But," he thought quickly, "we're not going to carry you home on our shoulders, just walk along with you."

Christy tried to stifle a laugh, but a corner smile seeped through. "Well, okay then."

"Hey, you … Tucker," a voice called from out of the darkness. "You guys think you're real funny, don't ya?"

"What are you talkin' about?" Tucker had no idea what was going on. Besides, the fellow didn't look right to him. What was it about him that seemed strange? The guy wasn't close enough to the streetlight to make out his face. It wasn't a Halloween mask. It was something else.

"Are you going to come down here and take your beating?" The guy in the shadows growled like a wolf at the edge of where civilized people live.

Tucker motioned to the other four. "We'd better go inside." He stood and waved them past.

"Runnin' away, are ya?" The dark figure, and the other two blobs, ran toward the house as Tucker and his friends darted into the house.

"No, you don't," the mouthy one demanded. "You're not going to get away so easy." He charged up to the door just as Gramma jerked it open.

"My goodness, boys. What happened to you?" she questioned with a caring grandmother's tone. Standing in front of her, just beyond the storm door, were three of the smelliest, slimiest, dirt-covered trio that ever stumbled around Dunlap.

"Well," Tucker began while studying the three. "If it isn't Vinny, Gus, and Morty. I should have smelled you three from a distance." Tucker looked past Vinny. The sky was bright as the full moon escaped the cover of clouds that blanketed above. "It looks like you guys fell in a mud puddle."

Grandpop and Uncle Jacob came to the door and stood there, providing shoulder-to-shoulder protection for their home. Tucker smiled as he remembered the Ezekiel verse about standing in the gap to close the hole in the city wall. "Good evening, Vinny," Uncle Jacob drew out slowly. "What's this all about?"

Vinnie grabbed the doorknob, still shaking with rage. "Your boy here heard me, and these two guys make plans today at school. We went out to knock over Harvey

Wallheiser's outhouse, and your precious Tucker beat us to it. He and these other four idiots pushed on it earlier in the evening and knocked it off its foundation."

"I did not," Christy protested. "My mother and I made cookies for the Halloween beggars."

"I wasn't even in Dunlap," Johnny announced firmly. "I live in Elkhart. I didn't get here until suppertime."

"So, when you three pushed on it …" Uncle Jacob didn't even have to finish his sentence. "I can see the picture already." He burst out laughing at the thought of it.

"We fell, head first, into the slop." Vinnie's growl was so loud, Carolyn came to the head of the stairs to see what was going on.

Grandpop smiled and shook his head in disgust. "Dummkopf."

Carolyn wasn't a tall person, but she was a determined one. "Gramma, do you want me to call the sheriff? Get these stink bombs out of here?"

"Well, now, Carolyn," Gramma paused and studied the boys up and down. "I'd say, that's up to Vinnie, wouldn't you, young man? Carolyn, these young men fell into an outhouse pit when they snuck in to work some mischief and knock it over." She turned sweetly back to the boys now standing at the door, covered in glop. "Wouldn't you say that explains it?"

Carolyn came down the steps, stood beside Gramma, and folded her arms. "Pee yew," she said as she covered her nose with her hand. "It smells like you three crawled through a barnyard. I'm sure you're uncomfortable. It seems to me you have two choices. You can go on home and take a nice hot bath—or you can sit in your filthy clothes in the county jail, with putrid, human waste caked all over you, and pull nasty bits of toilet paper out of your hair. It's up to you."

"What do you say, boys?" Uncle Jacob asked. "Seems to me to be an easy choice. But that may just be me and my comfort level. But we're going to respect your right to make it."

"I'm getting out of here." Morty squared his shoulders and turned. "I'm smarter than this."

"Me too," Gus defiantly announced as he stomped off. The gloppy sound of his shoes made Christy gag.

"And you?" Gramma asked Vinnie.

"I'm going home." Vinnie started to turn. "Please, Mrs. Moyer, don't call the sheriff. My dad would be so mad. He might make me live in these clothes for days."

"Well, now, Vinnie, I'll make a deal with you." It sounded to Tucker like Gramma was making one of her bargains. "I won't call the sheriff if you show up for church and Sunday school every Sunday from now through Thanksgiving."

"Yes, Ma'am." Vinnie slouched and dragged himself down the porch steps. It looked like he could hardly carry himself in the stiffening coat and pants.

"Wonder why he's so sad?" Tucker asked, mocking Vinny with a turned-down mouth.

"He's had a bad day," Christy joined in. As she watched the drying gunk fall off Vinny's shoes, she couldn't stop laughing.

"I've had a great day," Bobby giggled. Turning to Gramma, he asked, "May I use the bathroom?"

"Of course." Gramma took Grandpop by the arm. "It's past time to go to bed, Pa. Let's go up."

Tucker called after them. "We're going to walk Christy home."

"Oh, ja," Gramma turned and waved them out the door. "Ja, ja, that is the safe way after an evening like this."

"Doesn't Tucker make the days interesting?" Grandpop mumbled, shaking his head as they started up to their room.

Tucker watched as Bobby headed to the wall-hanging telephone near the side door. "What are you doing?"

Bobby set his eye on the phone and didn't change his direction. "I'm going to make a call on this contraption."

"Have you ever used a crank phone?" Tucker reached for the receiver. "Who ya callin'?"

"I thought I'd let my mom know I'm okay. I'll call Aunt Helen. She'll pass it on to Mother."

"Good." Tucker was relieved. He didn't want to betray the trust Bobby had in him, but he knew his brother's mother would be frantic by this time. Tucker picked up the candlestick receiver from the left side hook of the phone. Then he turned one long crank using the knob on the right. "Dalia, sorry it's late. Call Roger Hatzinger in Goshen, please." He handed his brother the receiver.

Bobby listened for the connection to pick up on the other end of the line. "Hi, this is Bobby."

Tucker heard the Dunlap side of the conversation. Bobby said very little. "I'm fine. I'll be back tomorrow. Don't worry." Then he hung up.

"Okay. I'll go into the bathroom and be right out."

Tucker went back onto the porch and searched the front yard. No one lurked behind the willow tree. The front yard was silent except for the crickets that persisted in their chirping. "No arguing about it, Christy. We're going to walk you home."

"I think I'd like that…this time." Christy looked at the yard and side street. Joe led the way down the porch steps. "Well, if Joe is going too, that settles it. With a war hero in the lead, we'll all be safe."

Bobby came out of the house and closed the door. "Okay, I'm ready to go along."

They all walked along Moyer Avenue, past the church and Stuart's house. Down in the next block, Etta turned off the porch light and called out, "Night, Tucker."

"Night, Etta," Tucker called back.

A little farther, Freddie announced he was home and peeled off from the group, "My house. See ya tomorrow," he added as he darted in through his front door.

"This has been a great evening, Tucker." Christy punched him lightly on the shoulder. "I always have fun when we're out and about."

"Nothing like this happens in town," Johnny agreed. "Home, school, church, and home again."

"Look, Christy," Tucker pointed out. "Your mom is watching for you at the door."

"Hi, Mom," Christy waved. "Gotta go in. Bobby, Johnny, will I see you two tomorrow?"

"Yep, you will." Johnny touched her shoulder. "Mom and I are staying with the Moyers tonight."

She ran up to the front door, then turned. "Hope it all works out for you and Bobby. Tucker, getting back into the house will be another adventure."

"No problem," Tucker called back with a chuckle. "Bobby," he began a review as they started walking back to the house. "Remember, swing up into the tree. Climb up the antenna, and grab the window ledge. I'll hurry upstairs and open the window."

The overhanging clouds had completely drifted on, leaving the night sky sparkling with the brightest stars Tucker could remember. Moonlight splashed across the street, adding light to their steps. It was easy for Tucker to forget the darkness from earlier in the evening that lurked in the shadows and waited on the edge of his loving home.

Beside the parsonage, Pastor Dailey pulled his son's bicycle around toward the garage. "It was a good Beggars' Night, Tucker."

"Sure was," Tucker said with a big grin. "Very … eventful."

"Very," Bobby added. "This was more fun than I ever had."

"More fun than mischief." Johnny shoved his hands in his pockets.

"More fun than pushing over the outhouse this afternoon if we had landed in the pit." Tucker suddenly realized just how perfect his day had been. "I agree. It was the most fun day of them all."

Chapter Twenty-Two
Camping in the Attic

"Remember, Bobby, flip your leg up over the limb of the tree." Tucker gave a quick reminder, then he and Johnny went around to the side door. Gramma usually left the Moyer Avenue door unlocked until Tucker was in for the night. His grandmother would expect two boys to come through the door: Tucker and Johnny, not Bobby, too.

Upstairs, Tucker stopped at the linen closet in the hall. He pulled out several blankets and a couple of down-filled pillows Gramma made from feathers Roman Swartz's wife, Ruth, gave her. Ruth traded the feathers for some hand cream Gramma bought from the Avon lady. Roman was an Amish delivery man who used to bring ice to Gramma's kitchen before the Moyer home got the new refrigerator. Handing the pillows to Johnny, he tucked the blankets under his arm. Halfway between the storage closet and Tucker's room, a well-worn floor plank squeaked a usual reminder that the house was not completely asleep.

Tucker found Bobby already waiting at the bedroom window, making a face at Johnny through the glass. Tucker raised the window and helped Bobby climb in. A finger to his lips reminded them all to be silent, followed by a crook of his finger, prompting them to follow.

They followed Tucker through the closet door in his room and up the attic stairs, to where they could quietly talk. He flipped on the switch and looked around. "We'll camp out up here."

Bobby looked around the space from one side to the other. He whispered, "Many of the homes in California are ranch-style, all on one floor with no attic."

Tucker scanned the many treasures around him. "No attic? Where do they put their stuff?"

"Stuff?" Bobby stopped and shrugged. "They don't have very much *stuff*. When they've finished with something, they throw it away."

"Throw it all away?" Tucker gulped and grabbed his shirt in pretend shock.

Bobby took a few steps toward a funny-looking low bench over toward the front of the house. It had three primitive legs and a leather pad for a seat.

Tucker pointed to the front of the attic. "Don't walk on that side, Bobby. That's over Gramma and Grandpop's room. They might hear you. The other side is over Tim's old room, now Sarah's bedroom, until she finds a job. Don't worry about that corner over there." Tucker pointed to the spot opposite the area over his room. "Carolyn will work late at the telephone office. She shares a room with Betsy. And Betsy will never hear anything. She could sleep through a train wreck even if it crashed in the front yard."

"What is all this stuff?" Bobby asked as he turned and surveyed all the stacks around him. Clothing hung on rods under the eaves, and trunks sat in a random assortment in the center— flat ones and hump-top beauties. Stacks of Uncle Jacobs books and magazines were everywhere.

Tucker shrugged and smiled. "All this stuff? It's our life."

"Those are National Geographic Magazines," Johnny pointed to the bundles of bright yellow periodicals that lined the narrow spots where the roof met the floor. "There are pictures of some of the towns in Europe hit the hardest during the war. I found one magazine with photos of Merkers in it. That's where a sniper killed my dad. I'd never seen those pictures before." The boys were quiet for a minute as the thought of Johnny's loss shrouded them.

Johnny broke the uncomfortable silence. "What is that?" He pointed to that same low bench-like thing. "I don't remember that was up here last year."

"Great-Uncle Frederick, Grandpop's brother, had it in his attic. He was cleaning things out to sell his house and was going to get rid of it. Uncle Jacob brought it home. Frederick is going to move in with his daughter, Alvera." Tucker walked over to an odd, old object, straddled the seat, and sat down. "Great-granddad's father was a cobbler. I think this bench was his."

"Your great-great-grandfather?" Bobby's surprise erupted with a dropped jaw and wide eyes.

"Yep. The family brought a bunch of stuff with them when they moved from Pennsylvania. I guess they couldn't leave part of their history behind." Tucker opened the drawer under the seat and took out some handmade tools: awls, some punches, a few scraps of leather, and a shoe hammer. "These are the cobbler's tools. The shoe lasts, are in this box. Lasts are the wooden molds around which the cobbler shapes the shoe." He pointed to an orange crate beside the bench. "There is also a cloth sack, or a poke as Grandpop would say, with tiny wooden pegs to hold the shoes together. 'A poke to tote them in,' is one of his favorite string of words."

Bobby touched one of the square-toed shoe molds. "It looks like it belongs in a museum."

Tucker nodded and smiled. "That's what an antique expert told us."

"This is a neat trunk." Bobby ran his fingers over the leather tooling on the rounded top and down the sides to the leather handles. It was a small, interesting old travel case. Tucker had been to the bottom of it many times.

"That old trunk just has pictures and stuff." Tucker showed Johnny and Christy its contents when they were up in the attic a year ago.

Bobby fingered the trunk latch. "Are there any I might like to see?"

"There are some pictures of your dad." Johnny looked at Tucker.

"My mom is in most of the pictures, too." Tucker looked away from Bobby and tried to think of something else.

"It's alright," Bobby whispered. "I know Dad was married to your mom first before she died. He's even married to someone else now."

Tucker tried to sound upbeat. It was getting too quiet in the attic. "Okay…sure. Dad married your mom, Martha, soon after my mom died. It's a sore subject in our house. I don't want to hurt your feelings, Bobby."

Tucker opened the lid carefully and lifted out the piece of paper on top of a stack of other letters and pictures. "This was the newspaper story about the assignation of President Abraham Lincoln. Grandpop was a little boy, but he remembers the day the information got to Pennsylvania. First, people heard that Booth shot Lincoln. Then they had to wait for a telegram stating that he died."

Johnny sighed deeply. "I don't remember seeing the old newspaper the last time I was up here."

"Here, Bobby. Here's a picture of Dad." Tucker handed his brother a high school picture of Sean McBride.

Bobby stared at the picture for a minute until a smile took over his face. "I remember him."

"I know he remembers you. That's for sure. He told me you were in town last year. Some of us started for Goshen. We got side-tracked. No, fast-tracked."

"Fast-tracked?"

Johnny looked at the picture, then at Bobby. "We found ourselves on the fast track many times. That often happens when we're around Tucker for very long. He's not afraid of height, depth, anything in, or anything out. But I gotta tell you, it's fun to hang around Tucker McBride."

Chapter Twenty-Three
Hiding in Plain Sight

When Tucker woke up, he found he was not in his bed. It wasn't a bed at all. He was on the rough, wood-planked floor in the attic. *"Right,"* he thought to himself, *"I remember. We camped out."* He looked around, and sure enough, Bobby and Johnny were still sleeping. They all stayed up late, talking, then slept in their clothes. Now, the sun was up. How was he going to get Bobby out of there? Everyone would see him going out the window, and he couldn't just walk downstairs. Wait, he had an idea.

Johnny stretched and yawned as he rubbed his eyes. "Hey, this was great. I like it up here."

"Me too." Bobby sat straight up and rubbed his neck. "Sleeping on the floor, my neck doesn't hurt."

"Good. Ask your step-father to put a board under your mattress. That's what Grandpop did when his neck hurt in the morning."

Bobby's eyes narrowed. "Okay, but you do know I'm not eighty-nine years old."

Tucker didn't answer. He stood up and looked out the attic window. "Bob, we may have a problem. Your plot to spend some time here won't work if you're not planning to go home after breakfast."

Bobby's face curled up in confusion. "Why?"

"Well, since the sun is up, my Grandpop and Gramma will be up too by now. You can't walk down through the living room on your way out. We're going to have to plan something else, so no one spots you. If you show up at the dining room table and you weren't here—"

"Can't I go back out your bedroom window? That's how I got up here. I'm getting good at this breaking-and-entering." Bobby looked down on the ground and out past the garden, laying silent under piles of leaves. "I don't see anyone down there."

Johnny chuckled and held his mouth to cover the sound. "With our luck, they'll probably all come outside when you're hanging from the windowsill. At least, that's the kind of thing that happens to us."

"You didn't break in, Bobby. You just came inside in a unique way." He paced back and forth for a few seconds. "Okay," Tucker brightened. "Let them see you." He hurried to the corner where another stack of newspapers Uncle Jacob forgot lay stacked. "Newspapers make the best cleaning cloths for windows, according to Gramma. We'll only pretend to have some water. Johnny, have you made peace with height?"

"I'm fine." He squinted a little in confusion. "If I hang around you long enough, I won't have a phobia in the world. What did you have in mind? Just how high does it have to be for you to call it *height*?"

"I'd say," Tucker grinned at John, "about as high as this house." He slowed down but paced another few seconds. "Come on. We'll hide Bobby out in the open." Tucker opened the attic windows over his room on the backside of the house. "I'll go out first. Bobby, you go out the other window, and Johnny, you man the widows to the right. We have to make sure they see Bobby. They expect to see you up here, Johnny, but not Bob."

The third floor, or attic of the house, was not as large as the second floor. It was part of the tall peaks of the house. It had two broad dormers in the roof, with two double-hung windows in each dormer. Once someone was out of the window, there was room for them to stand on the second story.

"Okay, guys, follow me." Tucker swung out the window, right leg first, and stood on the second-story roof. Bobby and Johnny followed him with whoops of laughter that Tucker hoped people heard at least to the stop sign. Pulling a sheet of newspaper from the stack they brought out with them, they turned around and began wiping the glass and window sills.

Tucker couldn't remember when he last washed the attic windows. That had been Tucker's job for several years. Grandpop used to climb outside and wash them. But Gramma wouldn't let him anymore. Tucker worked hard, but *washed* would be a stretch this time. Since there was no water involved, maybe cleaned was enough. Tucker could smell the dust that fell from the glass.

"What ya doin'?" Freddie stood on the ground with his hand shielding his eyes from the morning sun. "I don't see a bucket of water and vinegar up there."

"We're cleaning the windows." Tucker was calm and casual, yet loud enough to make sure his grandparents would hear him in the house.

When the screen door to the summer house banged, Tucker knew they had succeeded. "Tucker, my goodness," Gramma called out from the ground. "I meant to ask you to do that. I didn't know you were going to start this early in the morning. Some of the neighbors might still be sleeping." She covered her eyes and squinted. "What are you using for water?"

Tucker didn't answer that question. He created an explanation that went with a newly dreamed-up answer. "We were up here last night. The moon was bright, but the windows were so dirty, it was hard to see out. Norman came along just in time to help."

Gramma looked at the house, up and down. "How did he get up there?"

"Well, Gramma, if you truly want to know. You swing your leg up over that low branch of the tree there on the corner. Then shinny up Uncle Jerry's antenna pole. Next—"

"Never mind," Gramma interrupted. "I get the idea. You've used your Uncle Jerry's shortwave antenna for many things. But I don't plan to climb a tree or shinny up the side of a building." She looked the windows over and smiled. "I'll get out the cereal. Freddie, you might as well come in and eat some breakfast when you're finished. You too, Norman."

"Thanks, Gramma," Tucker laughed and gave a thumbs up to his friend. "I'll bring some water up the next time. Or, maybe I'll buy some of that new Windex spray. It'll be okay for now. The sun can shine through better than before. It's going to be a bright day."

Chapter Twenty-Four
Life Looks Different from the Sky

Since they acted like window washers, Tucker figured they might as well clean the dirt off the glass. Tucker and the boys finished the windows and came back into the attic. He grinned and gave them a thumbs up. "We did it."

"We sure did." Bobby stretched his leg through the attic window and brushed off his clothes. "Tucker, you have a lot of ideas."

"You should have been with us last summer." Johnny picked up his shoes from the floor, sat on the rough planks of the attic, and put them on. "We had quite an adventure."

"I smell something good." Bobby's nose tipped up as he seemed to follow a familiar aroma.

"Smells sweet," Tucker agreed as he sniffed the air. The three boys pounded down the attic steps through Tucker's closet, unconcerned about the noise. Since the window cleaning charade, they no longer needed to step lightly.

Downstairs, as they passed through the dining room, Bobby stopped and stared. He pointed to Betsy, stretched out on the hardwood floor that bordered the oriental carpet. "Is she okay?"

"Thanks for your concern, Norman," Betsy said with a patient grin. "I didn't fall or pass out. I washed my hair."

"On the floor?" Bobby's brows shot up nearly to his hairline.

"No," Tucker explained. "She washed her hair in the kitchen sink, then put a towel over the floor register where the heat rises and dries it. The towel keeps her long hair from going into the black register grate when she lies down on it." To Betsy, he teased, "I'm surprised you're up this early."

Betsy rolled her eyes. "I'm meeting friends later this morning, little brother. And Norman, Grandma helped wash my hair. She used the pitcher pump while I rinsed all the shampoo out. Then, I added a squirt of lemon juice for shine."

"Who would have thought?" Bobby shook his head. "I have no sisters in California. How would I know?"

Tucker squinted skeptically. "Bets, you usually wash your hair on Saturday night."

"Nancy Stuart and I walked around the neighborhood after Beggars' Night. Everyone had turned off their porch light. Joyce Dunlevy decorated the front of their house with a few bales of straw and a scarecrow to celebrate the harvest. Nancy and I saw some kids ripping into the scarecrow and one of the bales, throwing straw all over Dunlevy's yard and driveway. So, Nancy and I stopped them. That was after they threw straw all over us. It was thick in my hair."

Tucker brushed off his arms as if he were the one dressed like a scarecrow. "You went to bed covered in straw?"

"Of course not." Betsy pulled herself up on one elbow. "I combed out all the straw and brushed it off my clothes before I went to bed. But I had to wash the straw dust out of my hair this morning."

Gradually, Tucker's ears picked up on the other conversation in the room. He strained his attention to the dining room table. Gramma continued to explain to Sam how hard Sarah's last few years had been. They talked low as if they were gossiping about someone even though they sat at the table with them. Each held a steaming cup of coffee with a smokey aroma.

Gramma explained, "Steven was a lot older than Sarah. When he retired early because of his health, they moved out of their home. It was a parsonage, and they didn't own it. Sarah, still very young, was capable of teaching, but no jobs were available after the war." Gramma got up and brought the coffee pot to the table and a plate of buttered toast.

Tucker's mouth watered when he saw the honey pot on a plate to catch the drips, a jar of Gramma's grape jelly, and Gramma's homemade bread. Nothing could be better than Gramma's grape jelly. Well, maybe. His mother used to make grape juice for the communion services at church from the grapes in her yard. But Tucker was too little. He never got to taste any before she died.

"We're going to enjoy sweets this morning." Goldie handed Tucker a plate loaded with a sliced loaf of Amish Friendship Bread*. "I brought this out to thank Rebecca for teaching our ladies how to make mincemeat." She looked at the plate of bread, butter, and jam. "A well-balanced breakfast," she said with a smile. "Bread…and bread."

"The Amish bread looks so moist and sweet." Tucker's mouth watered over the dark, nutty treat. It smelled terrific.

"It's the starter." Goldie inhaled and placed a piece of the sweet cinnamon and sugar-topped bread on Tucker's plate. "It has a wonderful, yeasty smell. Like, when you drive by a bread company early in the morning and smell the glorious scent of the rising bread."

Gramma sat down with her coffee and two slices of bread, one of each. "Sarah lived in a parsonage during her entire marriage. Every church Steven served provided a home and utilities. She and Steven never owned a home of their own. Sarah never got to sew curtains for the kitchen or pick out the wallpaper that hung in the dining room or choose the color of the carpet. Sarah's entire married life, she walked on beige rugs. Some of the parsonages had wonderful parlors where Steven and Sarah could greet people who would stop in on Sunday afternoon to visit. The house the church provided usually had four large bedrooms in anticipation of a large family. But the Lord chose not to bless them that way. Steven didn't make a lot of money, so buying their own home wasn't even a possibility." She took a bite of Goldie's bread and closed her eyes. "Goldie, this is wonderful. I didn't know they had Amish families in Elkhart. Where did you get this delicious recipe?"

"Well, that's for sure," she said with a laugh. "There are no Amish farms in town. My friend Anna gave me the recipe. Her grandmother was born Amish. She shared the recipe with the gals in the Ladies Aid Society."

Sam nodded. "Becca's right. And preachers don't make enough money to save for a down payment."

Grandpop just shook his head. "Still, they didn't spend one night out in the open under the stars or tucked away in the shivering cold in a makeshift tent as some had done during the depression. Das ist gut.*"

Tucker reached across the table, took a thick slice of Gramma's toast, and drizzled honey across the top. "Help yourself, guys. Gramma's bread is the best."

"So, what did you do?" Sam called to Sarah as she came back into the room. Sam poured a second cup of coffee and topped it off with a bit of cream.

Sarah carried a round of cheese and a sharp knife from the kitchen. "The only thing we could do." She shrugged and sliced off pieces of cheese. "Have a little protein with your bread," she offered. "Ralph Wagoner, a member of our last congregation, offered us an affordable, available apartment for Steven's retirement years. I told my husband I wasn't sure about it." Sarah shook her head. "I said, with the two-year lease he's requiring, what if we come to a point where we can't afford to stay there?"

Steven said, "I think we'll be okay. You sign here below my signature." She got up as the boys asked for a second piece of toast. "Steven's confidence was contagious. His warm but worn-out expression could coax the most stubborn parishioner into a compromise position on any topic."

Gramma patted Sarah's hand and reminded her, "You had schooling but no real-life experience when you got married, Sarah."

"You went to college, right, Sarah?" Tucker was amazed. A woman in his family had gone to college.

Sarah smiled. "Ball State Normal College in Muncie. I went for two years and earned my teaching certificate. I wanted to teach children in the elementary grades. I experienced living away from home and making decisions on my own. But, when I met and married Steven Harter, I gave up my dream of teaching. The wife of a pastor doesn't work outside the home."

"Why?" Tucker couldn't see what marrying a pastor had to do with not working. During the war, many mothers and other women in Dunlap either worked in an office, a factory, the classroom or volunteered their time with the Red Cross or the many other places that needed willing hands.

Sarah looked up and thought. "I have no idea, Tucker. Why don't more women work? Isn't it silly?" She folded her handkerchief until it formed a hankie, babes-in-a-blanket*. "When we retired, Mr. Wagoner said, 'Now, don't you two worry about it. We've known each other for a long time. If you need to get out of the lease at any time, just let me know.' With that promise, we signed the lease. Ralph Wagoner folded the paper and put it in his pocket. Steven died the next year."

Tucker thought everything seemed a little heavy to him. Maybe he and the guys should get out of the house. When there was a knock on the door, it was a good excuse for Tucker to break up all the sadness. "Christy, come in. We were just thinking of going back up to the airport. Walter Crompton said he'd go up today. He said he'd give us a plane ride."

"Us?" Christy asked.

Tucker was aware Christy knew him well. "He was talking to me, but he knows I usually have someone with me." He smiled. "Most of the time, it's you."

Outside, they all piled into Tucker's Model A. They decided who would sit where, by body size. Tucker, Christy, and Johnny were in the front. Bobby and Freddie were in the rumble seat. Off they went.

Late October can be cold in northern Indiana. In some years, snow would fall on the pumpkins in the yard and the scarecrows in the fields. That morning, the geese were still flying south overhead with honks of joy for their migration. Tucker wondered if Bobby and Freddie in the back would freeze by the time they got to the airport. Since he wasn't old enough to have a driver's license, they needed to stay off the highway. To avoid traffic, they took the back roads, through the country. It took a little longer, but fewer county police traveled those roads.

When they got to the Midway Airport, they bounced and rattled over the grass and uneven ground of the area not set aside for the runway. Tucker had no rearview mirror in the A Model. But he could feel the jolts and bolts of the two boys in the back.

"Hi, kid," Walter called out when Tucker pulled the old car into the smooth grass of the airport runway. "You have two loads there. I can only take three at a time."

"Yep, Bobby, Christy, and I will go up together and then Johnny and Freddie." He motioned to Johnny. "Why don't you two go up first."

The ride wouldn't be a long one. Just a spin around the airport, the school, and the streets around Dunlap so they could look down on their home. Johnny and Freddie looked at the plane and took a deep breath.

Mr. Crompton looked at the first co-pilot with a wary eye. "You two ever fly before?"

"Nope," they chimed in together.

"Okay." Walter lowered his head and looked at the bunch from under his thick, hairy eyebrows. "Sit still, talk calmly, stay quiet, and keep your hands off the rudder control, where the stick goes. That's how I steer this bird."

"Yes, Sir," Bobby announced.

When the first two got in the cockpit with Walter, buckled up, and taxied down the grass runway, Tucker walked over to the hanger where Rex Martin stored his airplane. There was an old bench beside the door.

"I was riding with Rex a little over a year ago when he wrecked his airplane," Tucker said when he looked in the window of the hanger. "Wow! What a ride."

Bobby laughed and shook his head. "Are you always wrecking, or climbing, or dangling from something?"

Before Tucker could open his mouth, Christy answered for him. "Yes, yes, he is."

"Well, maybe," Tucker reluctantly admitted with a sparkle in his eye. "Bobby, what do you do on the weekend?"

"My step-dad has taken me and some friends to a bowling alley a few times. I like that. I'm pretty good at bowling. And the hot dogs at the alley lunch counter are great, smothered in mustard and onions." He licked his lips like he was enjoying the memory of the long sandwich. "With school and all, I'm busy."

"Bowling?" Tucker beamed. "That sounds like fun."

"Tucker—" Bobby slowly put some words together. "What was all of that? Your grandmother's cousin was talking about something?"

"It has been hard for Sarah." Tucker did worry about Sarah. Gramma and Grandpop talked about her situation often. He just didn't like to think about things he couldn't fix. So, he would stop trying to find answers for her when there seemed to be no answers out there. "Not only did her husband die last year, but she lost the income he brought in, too."

"Can't she get a job?" Bobby also found himself caught up in the quest for a solution. "Out in California, a lot of women work."

"Now that all the boys are back from the war, it's hard."

Bobby's face twisted in a question. "There were teachers in the war?"

Tucker looked at him in disbelief. "Grandpop listens to the news every evening. Bobby, millions of Americans served in the United States Armed Forces during the war. Over sixteen million. I imagine some of them had been teachers."

Bobby ignored Tucker's expression. "Maybe as more of the G.I.s get married, there will be some open jobs. Many women gave up their work to returning soldiers. That opened up jobs for others."

Christy pointed to the approaching aircraft. "They're coming back already. I can hear the whir of the wings." Then, they heard the screech of the brakes.

When the plane taxied to a stop, Freddie got out, holding his stomach. "I almost got sick, Johnny. We had him cut the ride a little short."

"At least you got your first airplane ride … ever." Tucker patted both of the guys on the back.

Walter got out, stretched, and checked his watch. "You three about ready?"

"We sure are." Tucker and the other two piled into the cockpit. He took the co-pilot's seat in the front.

"Okay," Walter began a checklist of his own making. It wasn't for a co-pilot. It was for Tucker, the most active kid most people in Dunlap knew.

Tucker showed Bobby and Christy how to secure themselves with the seat strap as Mr. Crompton began his drill. "Talk calmly and stay relaxed. Enjoy the ride, but don't touch that." He pointed to the top of a stick that came up from its attachment on the floor. "Don't put your hands on any part of it. Tucker, don't even look at it."

"No, Siree," Tucker gave in. "I won't even put my little finger on it."

Walter taxied the plane down the bumpy runway again and soon lifted off into the late morning sky. As they took to the air, the sky got big and wide until Walt used the untouchable stick to level off.

"Look down," Tucker said over his shoulder to Bobby and Christy in the back seat.

"I thought I wouldn't want to," Christy admitted. "But it's beautiful, all the golds and reds of the fall leaves. Look, there's Yellow Creek. See how it wiggles like a snake?"

"I like the size of everything down there on the ground." Bobby pressed his nose against the window. "It all looks so little."

Tucker could see out the side window from the front seat, even though the pilot had to keep the nose up. "Look, there's the church," Tucker marveled as he looked down at the red brick building that he knew as well as his own home. "So … that's our house across the side street."

Christy got excited. "You can see mine from here, too. Just a few houses down the road and around the corner from yours."

"Let's go back," Walt announced and reached for the control stick. He pulled back, but the plane didn't shift position. Again, Mr. Crompton pulled on the control stick. Nothing happened when he moved it again and again. He appeared to struggle more with the control stick. It should have moved easily but, it seemed stuck. But how?

Suddenly, Walter's voice filled the cockpit. "Tucker!" he bellowed. "Get your foot away from the base of the control stick."

Tucker laughed mischievously. "I didn't touch it. I kept my hands on my legs for all to see."

"Not with your hands," Walt shouted. "You wedged your feet up against the stick."

Tucker pulled himself up straight and tried to act mature. After all, Walter had trusted him to sit in the front. But he had to admit he loved to tease. Tucker claimed his hand did not touch the control stick. Hand or their foot, it didn't matter.

Chapter Twenty-Five
A Fire Can Bring Out Good Things

They were on their way home when the sorrowful whale of a fire department ambulance filled the air. The firetruck had already come from the center of Elkhart to put out a fire somewhere in Dunlap. The siren wound up and down the scale, calling people to their windows to see the sleek ambulance pass.

"Wonder where they're going?" Christy thought aloud as the Model A neared the Moyer intersection.

"Let's find out." Tucker turned right and followed the fire truck out and over the tracks. "This is the road Dad lives on." He knew he was on a major road without a driver's license. He also knew County police would be around any burning building. But his curiosity far outweighed his caution – as usual.

"Oh no," Bobby gasped. "Maybe he'll see me."

Christy sat back and looked at her new friend. "Do you think anyone would recognize you in that get-up, wig, hat, sunglasses? Especially one who hasn't seen you in several years?"

"Probably not." Bobby turned and looked beyond the window. "You're right." His voice became soft and distant. "It's been a long time."

It was October, but no clouds flew overhead like streams of cotton. The siren pierced through that ash-filled sky like an arrow shot from a bow. Tucker waved at Elmer Glug as he raked leaves. His yard had three of that kind of tree that refuses to drop their foliage all at once. Elmer waved the rake back and tipped his hat.

"Do you know everybody?" Bobby watched the man go back to his raking and added, "Is there anyone you don't know?"

"Not here in Dunlap. I think I know everyone." When the street took a slight bend to the east, Tucker lowered his head and squinted into the sun. "What is that?"

Christy put her hand up to her forehead to shield her eyes. "That looks like a child," she gasped.

"A little kid in the middle of the road?" Bobby stretched and tried to see. "The windshield is too dirty to see her, Tucker."

"Slow down, slow down," Christy yelled. "She's not just standing in the street. She's running toward us. She's not going to get out of the way."

The Model A slowed as the little curly-haired girl ran toward them. Tears streamed down her face. Tucker thought she couldn't have been more than three years old. Christy jumped out of the car and gathered the child in her arms.

"The fire's hot," the little miss sobbed as she rubbed her hand. "I can't find Mommy."

"Well, you're safe now." Tucker's heart ached for her. He wondered if the fire claimed her mother?

"Um-hum." The little girl held her hand away from her body as she snuggled close to Christy.

"You have an ouchy boo-boo, don't you? Let me see it." Christy gently unfolded the little one's hand. She looked at Tucker and shook her head. "You tell Tucker, you need to get some medicine on your hand."

"Gramma would have some Grandma Hooley Salve at the house. But we should ask the little girl's mom first."

"What if...?" Christy stopped in mid-question and gave the little one another hug.

"We have to find out," Bobby said as he tried to make room for the child. "We can't just drive off with someone's kid."

"You're right, Bobby." Tucker started moving the car slowly down the road. "Christy, why don't you stay in the car with the little girl while we check things out?"

"I don't think so," Christy said. "I don't see how I can keep her in the car."

As they neared the house, they saw flames leaping out of one of the upstairs windows. Dark smoke billowed up, blackening the sky. The fire department's pumper engine was already drowning the leaping blaze with water.

Tucker began to move the car in closer as they neared the area. Pulling over to the side of the road, he studied the situation from a distance. "I'd better leave the car here. I don't have a driver's license."

From a block away, they could see what was happening at the house. It was next to Sean's, with space for a garden between the two homes, and close enough for flying ashes to land in his yard. Firefighters were already working inside the house, leaving the front door open. Smoke seeped out and caught a low air current that quickly rose above the house.

"Are you sure you guys want to get closer, Christy? That's Kathy Marie's house," Tucker cautioned.

"Kathy Marie Riley?" Christy asked in disbelief.

"My Kathy," the little girl said, excitedly twisting to see her home.

"And you are …?" Christy asked.

"Charlotte."

"Um-huh." Tucker opened his car door. "I'm getting out."

Bobby jumped out on the passenger side. Balancing himself on the ditch side of the car, he maneuvered up onto the pavement.

Christy waited in the car with the little girl but held her breath as she watched the firefighters from the window. "Let's not look at that," she lightly touched the child's face, trying to redirect her gaze. "Let's try a game. I spy something red." She looked at a red lawn chair in the neighbor's yard.

"Umm," the short one looked around.

Johnny and Freddie slowly got out of the rumble seat. "Whose house is burning?" Freddie asked as they approached.

Christy leaned out of the window and put her hand on Freddie's shoulder as he passed. "I'm sorry, Freddie. It's the Riley home. Kathy Marie lives here." She knew Freddie had been close to Kathy Marie before Anna Fredrick caught his eye.

"Oh no." Freddie hurried toward the house, covering the pavement in huge strides. The others followed.

"Which one is Dad's?" Bobby asked as he pulled the bill of his ball cap down farther over his eyes.

Tucker raised his little finger and pointed toward the first house on the left before getting to Riley's. Their dad was in the yard. Tucker winced inside when Sean turned toward them.

"Tucker," Sean moved closer. "Stay away from the fire."

Tucker didn't think his dad had a right to tell him what to do. He didn't raise him; he wasn't even around much. Tucker saw himself as an independent adult. He didn't take orders from his dad, but he didn't argue with him either. Recently, they made peace with their anger.

"My friend lives here," Freddie called out but kept on walking. "Did anyone get hurt?"

"I don't think so. I see the fire chief called for an ambulance." Sean took a few steps in their direction. "But I think that was just a precaution."

"Oh no," Bobby whispered under his breath when Sean moved toward them.

"We're going to get a little closer." Tucker kept walking. "I'll let you know what I find out."

As they neared the house, Tucker couldn't believe what he saw. The Riley family always kept their home and yard immaculate. Virginia Riley not only kept the inside of the home fresh and full of life, but the outside was the most attractive house on the block.

The Riley's even white-washed the large rocks that bordered the little flower garden at the front of the house. That's what Amish families do. Now, smoke from the fire had turned the stones a dingy grey. Dark streaks from the water ran down the sidewalk.

The orange and yellow mums that happily bloomed regardless of frost didn't win the battle with the fire hoses. Trampled and crushed, they joined the list of damaged beauty around the yard. Two fancy porch rockers lay upside down, one with a broken rail. Curtains flapped out of shattered windows. Fancy pillows, pottery lamps, and once-white lampshades lay scattered in the water that ran out the front door.

"Hi," Tucker greeted the fireman who stood at the end of the driveway. "Anybody hurt?"

Freddie's eyes, drawn with fear, searched the house. "Is Kathy Marie alright?"

The fire chief smiled. "She's right over there."

Tucker and his friends hurried over to where Kathy was sitting on an old tree swing. The heavy ropes, suspended from a low hanging branch, held the two-inch-thick hickory-board seat. Kathy hung onto the ropes and let the autumn wind move and twirl her at its will.

The air was thick with ash and smoke. Tiny fragments of the Riley family's life drifted their way and stung their eyes.

Freddie asked softly, "Kathy, can we do anything for you?"

"The firetruck got here in time. We didn't lose too much. But we can't find Charlotte. I don't know what to do or where to go. The police should get here in a few minutes." She looked at the house. "It's all wet. Our whole lives drowned."

Tucker looked at the front of the house, where Mrs. Riley seemed dazed. She was straightening the boxwood shrubs trampled by the firefighters. But Tucker could see her hands shaking when Mrs. Riley stopped to rub her eyes. She stood slowly, straightening what seemed to be an aching back, then collapsed to her knees.

"I hear the police coming," Kathy said as she jumped out of the swing. "Charlotte is missing; they'll find her."

"No," Bobby assured her. "We saw her walking down the road and brought her back. She's over there in Tucker's Model A with Christy Tree."

"Oh, thank goodness. Thank you. Thank you." As she ran to the old car, she shouted. "Mom, Charlotte is over here."

Mrs. Riley yelled, "Vern, Charlotte is here!" She followed Kathy, Tucker, and the boys to the old car.

"Baby!" Mrs. Riley burst out when she saw Charlotte.

"Mommy!" The little hands reached out, carefully protecting her burned palm from touching anything.

"Char-Char." Her daddy put his arms around her and hung on.

Tucker wondered what it would feel like to have a mom and dad hug him. Would they be as happy if someone found him? But Gramma always said, "All the saints in Heaven will be glad you finally made it there, Tucker. They'll all greet you with hugs and hallelujahs." He smiled to himself and guessed Gramma was right.

When Vern Riley looked up, Tucker asked, "Is there going to be much damage to the house?"

Vern's sighs were deep and tired. "Everything will have to be cleaned and dried out after the firehoses do their job. Virginia is worried about some of our family pictures. Our wedding picture and our oldest daughter's graduation portrait are soaked."

Freddie hadn't said much. He wasn't a big talker on any day. When there was a tragedy or other problem, his mouth barely opened. But he knew Kathy. "Sorry, your house caught on fire."

They walked back toward the house. "How did it start?" Tucker asked but couldn't help thinking of Vinny and his three clowns. He saw that Mr. Riley had tried to push his brown leather recliner chair out the front door. There it sat, stuck in the opening.

Vernon Riley hurried back to his task. He climbed up over the arm of the chair, got behind it, and shoved so hard he nearly laid out flat on the porch floor.

Virginia sighed weakly. "Braxton was lighting matches in the wastepaper basket in his room." Tucker thought Kathy's mother looked exhausted, and it wasn't even lunchtime yet. "We can help clean things. Get all the smoke and dirt off of stuff," Tucker volunteered.

"Thanks, Tucker." Mr. Riley drug himself over to the big tree where the swing hung. "I think we'll have to let things dry out before we can clean it up."

"I can ask Noah Dominick if you can put things in his barn." Tucker knew Noah would help. He helped everyone. "Noah's pretty much not using the barn anymore. He doesn't farm, and the Model A he stored in there is sitting in your lane." He pointed his thumb over his shoulder.

"Right," Bobby joined in. "That way, everything will dry before some rain gets it wet all over again." He smiled like he was part of the solution. "A corner of my church burned a few years ago. They lined up all the hymnals on a long table in a neighbor's basement. Every day, someone would go down and turn the pages so they wouldn't stick together."

Mr. Riley's expression brightened. "What a great idea. What church do you go to?"

"Uh," Bobby tensed.

Tucker jumped in fast. "Norman just moved to town. That was his old church. His family hasn't picked a new one yet."

"Oh." Vernon Riley sighed. "Can you call Noah, Tucker? Our phone is out."

"Noah who, Vern," Virginia joined the group.

"Noah Dominick." Christy moved excitedly in anticipation of a real solution to what had seemed like an impossible situation. "Tucker is going to ask him if you can use his empty barn to store your stuff while it dries."

"Oh, Tucker, yes, thank you." Virginia was so excited she grabbed Tucker by both shoulders. "Go over to your dad's and use his phone to call Noah right now."

Tucker shot a glance at Bobby and shrugged questioningly. "Well …"

"Sure, Tucker," Bobby slapped him on the back. "I'll stay here and help them take some stuff out of the house. I'll be right here."

Jogging over to his dad's house across the street gave Tucker a few seconds to think. What if his dad asked about Bobby? Tucker knew how his brother's mom and aunt would worry. Maybe even more than worry. He knew how sad he was when Joe didn't get to come home after the war. He grieved more than he even knew until Uncle Jacob made some phone calls and brought the hero home. And Joe is a dog, not somebody's son.

"What did you find out?" Sean asked.

Tucker looked around quickly at his dad's place. The shingle siding was drab but unbroken, and Sean trimmed the grass nicely. Since Sean McBride didn't raise Tucker and his brother and sisters after their mother died, Sean's house never felt like home. At least, not to Tucker. *Home* was on the corner of South Main Street and Moyer Avenue.

"No one got hurt," Tucker answered, still over-stimulated by the fire and all he had seen. "So that's good."

"Thank goodness," Sean said and exhaled deeply.

Tucker wondered if "thank goodness" just meant "they were lucky." Did his dad ever really thank God for his blessings? "I need to use your phone." Tucker started for the house.

Sean followed him into the house. "Sure, what's going on?"

Walking through the back door, they entered a well-organized kitchen. On the corner of the counter, Tucker saw some baby diapers, clean and folded. He stopped a minute. "How's the baby?" He didn't wait for an answer. Over at the wall-hanging telephone, he took the receiver off the hook on the side of the phone box.

Sean ran his fingers over the stack of white cloth diapers. "Polly took him to the doctor for a checkup." He looked out the kitchen window above the sink. "Bobby is still missing, you know. His mom is worried sick. I can't believe he's gone."

Tucker slowly replaced the candlestick receiver on the hook. "I bet his mom is wild with worry. But I imagine Bobby will show up soon. It's time."

"Time?" Sean's forehead furrowed. "Have you seen him?"

"If I see him, I'll send him home … or wherever he's staying." Tucker picked up the receiver again. "Hi, Dalia. Please ring Noah Dominick's house." Tucker waited while the operator connected his dad's line to old Noah's. "Good morning, Mr. Dominick. This is Tucker McBride. Say, Vernon and Virginia Riley's house caught on fire this morning." He paused. "Yes, it is sad. But luckily, the flames didn't reach very much. But the living room furniture does have some smoke and water damage from the firehoses. Family pictures and stuff like that have to dry out. I wondered if they could use your barn to spread everything out and hang stuff up to dry. You're just down the road from their house."

Tucker could tell that his dad was listening. He was glad his dad was interested in his neighbors.

"Great, Noah," Tucker responded to Mr. Dominick on the phone. "Thanks. They'll get some help and bring the things down soon. Thanks again." Tucker replaced the receiver on the hook. "That's super," he said as he looked up at the clock and winced. "It's nearly lunchtime." He started for the door. "Thanks, Dad."

He hurried back over to Kathy Marie's house. Kathy sat again on the swing, pumping a little faster. Her dad lay on the ground with his knees up. Mr. Riley seemed to be storing up energy for the next task. Kathy's brother, Braxton, sat cross-legged beside him. Braxton drew frowning, sad faces in the dirt with a hickory stick. Charlotte clung to her mother's arms. Tucker wondered if *Char-Char* feared she'd lose her momma again. With all the sad, afraid, worried emotions around him, Tucker took a deep breath and announced, "It's all set."

Vern jumped up off the ground and gave Tucker a bear hug. "You did it, Tucker."

"Maybe some of your neighbors can help move your things down there." He looked at his Model A. "We could put some lamps and pictures in the rumble seat and unload them in the barn."

Virginia seemed to perk up. Her eyes brightened, and her wilted back straightened. "We'll somehow get the dining room and kitchen tables and chairs to the barn. Then we can spread out all the photos and lamps on top of them."

"I can stack a few chairs at a time in the rumble seat and make as many trips as necessary." Tucker slapped Mr. Riley on the back.

"Come on, Kathy." Christy grabbed her hand and pulled her friend off the swing. "With the four of us, plus you, we can get around the kitchen table and carry it down to the barn."

Riley's neighbor, Edgar, came over from the house next door. "I've heard about your great ideas. We'll load up my Ford truck with the heavier dining room table, the couch, beds, and chairs and get them down to the barn."

"The beds didn't get any of the water," Virginia added.

Vernon put his arm around his wife's shoulder. "They'll pick up the smell of all that smoke. In the barn, they can air out." He stopped and asked Tucker, "Do you think Noah would let us sleep in his barn? It would sure help to be close to the house and all our stuff."

"I'll bet he would," Tucker agreed as he started for his old car. He wanted to bring it closer for loading.

Quickly, the three boys, plus Christy and Kathy, hurried into the house, stumbled into the kitchen, and surrounded the Formica top table. Christy gave the command. "On my call of three…one, two, three." In unison, they lifted the table and started outside through the back door. "Step, step, step," she announced the cadence. They matched stride for stride and had already moved down off the back stoop when Tucker returned with the Model A.

Edgar pulled his shiny red truck into the yard and backed it up to the porch. "Load it up." Ed laughed, jumped out of the cab, and began to help Vern lift the flower-covered couch into the truck bed. "Dining room table next," he directed. "Heavy things have to be upfront, near the cab."

Tucker looked toward Noah's small farm. First, his team loaded the kitchen table onto Ed's truck. Now, they had gotten to the barnyard with living room lamps and were almost to the worn red, barn wood door. When they disappeared inside, Tucker breathed a relief. The very first step in the save-the-Riley's-stuff plan was finally in place.

He loaded the last pictures, table cloths, embroidered couch pillows, and light fixtures and headed for the dry, sweet, hay-smelling barn.

Chapter Twenty-Six
It Took the Whole Family

The Riley family's neighbors from up and down the road helped load the household goods and furnishings onto Ed's truck. It took several trips back and forth between the smoke-filled home and the airy red barn before Tucker and friends moved everything that needed moving. The double-wide barn doors slid open along their track and provided the front door air to match the breeze coming in the wide back door.

When Tucker and Bobby finally got home from the Riley fire, a surprise awaited them. As he pulled the old A Model up beside his house, several other cars dotted the side street. Tucker didn't recognize any of them, which was unusual. He could name the owner of most any car that passed in front of the house on a lazy Saturday afternoon. "Wonder what's happening."

Freddie and Johnny piled out of the rumble seat. Freddie stretched and stomped as a Charlie-horse grabbed the calf of his right leg like the claws of a plumber's wrench. He limped around the side of the car, grabbed the driver-side window, and leaned in. "What's going on? Why all the fuss?"

Tucker looked at the cars and pointed to a license plate. "That Chevy is from Goshen."

Bobby's face paled. "It sure is. The dark blue car is like the one Uncle Roger drives."

Freddie hobbled back as Tucker got out of the car. "Bobby, do you want to come over to my house until Tucker lets us know what's going on? You're welcome too, Johnny.

It might be better than walking in on something. I don't like surprises."

"Thanks," Johnny started toward the house. "But I think Mom wanted to leave this morning after she and Mrs. Moyer finished canning the mincemeat."

"Well, come on down, Johnny, if your mom isn't ready." Freddie and Bobby started hiking in the direction of Freddie's home.

"I'll see you later," Christy waved. "It's about lunchtime. I'm going home."

Tucker and Johnny went up the steps to the side porch and in the door. Goldie Washington was wiping off the countertop in the kitchen while Gramma dried the Ball canning jars full of mincemeat.

"Ah, Tucker," Gramma said as she went into the dining room. "You can help Mrs. Washington and John carry her jars of mincemeat out to her car. Your brother Bobby's mother called. She's coming over." She took hold of Tucker's arm. "Tucker, his mom is worried. Then, the strangest thing happened. Bobby called last night from this house." She looked him squarely in the eyes. "Now, how do you suppose that happened?"

"Because he called from here," Tucker admitted. He didn't lie to his grandmother when she asked him a direct question. "Now, don't get mad. Bobby wanted to spend some time in Dunlap, with me."

Gramma brushed the hair off her forehead. "He would have been welcome here. You know that."

"You did make him welcome, Gramma." Tucker looked down at the floor. "You gave him supper last night."

Gramma's mouth dropped. "How is that possible?"

Tucker smiled sheepishly. "You served him Stroganoff."

"Norman?" She covered her mouth in surprise, then changed her expression to a laugh. "I wondered why his haircut looked so funny."

Tucker peeked into the living room. "Someone else is here."

Sam came through the dining room on his way to the coffee pot to refresh his cup. "Hi, Tucker. Hot stuff in there."

"Hot stuff?"

"Ralph Wagoner is here to talk to Sarah. She called her attorney and asked him to come over too."

Gramma peaked in that direction. "I never knew Ralph was such a shyster."

"Thanks again, Rebecca," Goldie said as she gave Gramma a big hug. "This has been wonderful. Our church ladies will love making mincemeat from your recipe. It will be a big seller at our Christmas Bazaar. Now, you make sure Jacob or Carolyn brings you. It's the last Saturday in November."

"I wouldn't miss it. And Carolyn is always looking for tea towels and pillows for her new home once she's married." Gramma reached for a sack of mincemeat jars, but Tucker stopped her.

"No, Gramma. I've got it." Tucker took the sack that his grandmother held and followed Mrs. Washington out to her car. Johnny carried the extra meat grinder his mom brought and helped load up the car. Tucker waved and started back to the house. "Bye, Johnny. Glad you came. We had some Beggars' Night."

"The best ever," Johnny called after him.

As Tucker came back inside, Sam grabbed the coffee pot and began to make more coffee. He studied the bottom of the pot. A few grounds dotted the glass when he started to laugh. "I remember a toe-headed little Ralphie Wagoner running home after a friend of mine, Bill Blankenship, and I finally untied him from a tree and set him free. It had been our original plan to build a fire under the kid, just like we'd seen in the movies. Each of us was only nine years old. We were going to ignite the bonfire under him with matches we had pilfered* from behind the cross on the altar of the church over on Vine Street. Pastor Dinwiddie stored a book of matches there ever since he had a problem finding some when it was time to light the acolytes' tapers."

"Ralphie?" Tucker cringed when he thought about Ralph's son Vinny and the trouble he caused on Beggars' night.

"Little Ralphie wasn't always so aggressive," Sam snickered as he expanded the story. "That day at the almost bonfire, he ran home to Mama."

"Oh, Sam Treadway." Gramma squeezed his cheek a little. "You are such a rascal."

Tucker stood back. He didn't want to appear nosey, but he wanted to be supportive. And, to be honest, Tucker always knew what was happening at home.

In the living room, Sarah nearly whispered. "After Steven died, the family helped me move into one of your efficiency apartments, Ralph. That house is just a few doors north of here. There was a small refrigerator under a short length of counter, an equally small oven, and a two-burner hot plate." She glared briefly at Ralph.

"You said it was comfortable." Wagoner reminded her with a superior pinched-face look.

"It was. There was a murphy-bed that pulled out of the wall and a couple of chairs. It was nice to have a roof over my head, and that roof was close to family."

Tucker remembered too. It was the talk at the dinner table. But when Sarah couldn't afford to continue to live in the small apartment, she finally moved in with Rebecca, Joseph, and the kids. Then soon after the Fourth of July, 1946, Sarah received a letter from Wagoner. Tucker was fascinated by the fancy wording.

> *"As per your lease, you are still liable for*
> *the rent due for the last month you lived*
> *in the apartment, plus for the months*
> *after you moved out, until the end of*
> *the lease in December 1946."*

Again, Sarah passed the letter around the group that morning. The total of all rent payments due to Ralph Wagoner glared from the deceptively pure white paper. Sarah even let Tucker read it, but he couldn't grasp the meaning of the words on the paper. Everyone, except Wagoner, sat silently in the parlor.

Sarah was unable to pay any of it. After Steven died, she moved from the larger apartment she shared with her husband to the smaller one. It was all impossible. With her husband's small pension now dwindling to near-nothing, she couldn't afford to pay for the smaller one either. Now, Wagoner charged her for the one-month back-rent she couldn't afford to pay when she still lived there, plus the five months of rent remaining on the lease from August to December of 1946.

Wagoner was insistent. "Well, she was paying $16.50 a month for three and a half rooms. So, she owed for the last month she lived there and the remaining months to the end of the year."

Uncle Jacob took the paper and read it again and again, but the words didn't change. The letter was from the attorney who came with Ralph out to the house that Saturday.

Finally, Sarah spoke up in protest. "But Ralph, you told Steven and me you would release us from the lease whenever I needed to or wanted to. Your agreement extended to me, too."

"That's all well and good, Mrs. Harter," Attorney Smyth explained again. "But the lease is quite clear and must be honored. You signed it. It was the rental agreement to the larger apartment you were told you could get out of." He was growing impatient and sounded rude. With his snippy attitude, he acted like he thought he was smarter than anyone else in the room. "It doesn't apply to the smaller one."

Sarah straightened her back and drew herself up as tall as possible. She was small but she wasn't weak. "I know

I signed the lease, but Ralph, you did not tell me that your kindness and generosity didn't extend to me too, just to Steven."

"But it isn't in writing, Ma'am," the lawyer protested.

Tucker couldn't believe that a businessman, like Mr. Wagoner, wouldn't be good to his word. For years, the only thing needed was a handshake to seal a contract. And, Tucker was learning to be a man of his word.

"The only evidence of any business arrangement between you and Mr. Wagoner, Mrs. Harter, is the lease itself. How do you intend to pay it off?" Mr. Smyth demanded. "I'll take a check today, or I'll file a lawsuit on Monday."

Tucker found himself stepping into the middle of what was none of his business. "She has no money, Mr. Smyth. None."

"I'm so sorry to hear of your difficulty, Mrs. Harter." Smyth poured on words like maple syrup.

"What about a deal, Mr. Smyth," Tucker burst in again. It was kinda fun to be the legal negotiator in the situation. "Lux Radio Theater always has two lawyers making a deal."

"Mrs. Harter's attorney isn't here, however." Mr. Smyth reminded everyone.

"Carolyn is upstairs." Tucker's mind was racing. He might be able to come up with a solution. "She has beautiful handwriting. She can write down what Mr. Wagoner and Sarah agree to. Then they can both sign it and date it."

"Are you planning to be an attorney someday, young man," Mr. Smyth asked.

Sam shook his head. "Since my share-crop farmer doesn't make his crop payment until after Thanksgiving, I have no money," Sam began. "I can go to the bank on Monday. There are no leans against my farm. I can have the entire ninety-nine dollars for you by Monday afternoon or in a few days after that if there is a delay."

Ralph Wagoner stood up. "That's too late. Mr. Smyth will file the suit on Monday morning. We are asking the court for Mrs. Harter's wedding rings in-lieu-of the cash."

Tucker couldn't believe what Smyth said. "You can't wait a few days?"

"Tucker," Gramma cautioned. "Now, let's be quiet and let Sarah take care of this."

"I know I shouldn't talk," Tucker admitted but didn't stop. "It seems to me; Sarah only owes rent for the time she lived there and couldn't pay."

"Even if you still have to have the entire ninety-nine dollars—" Sam had another solution. "I could sell Dakotah's Chief's Blanket. I could get the blanket and give it to you right now, Ralphie. It's worth a lot more than ninety-nine dollars."

"But Sam," Tucker couldn't believe what he was hearing, "you told Maria Garcia you would just *rent* the blanket from her. The blanket is still hers. You're teaching me about being a man of his word."

Sam was silent. But his face turned from hopefulness to helplessness as his expression drooped.

Betsy had slipped down the steps and stood leaning on the pocket door that led into the parlor. She listened carefully to the conversation. "I've saved five dollars from babysitting. I can give Sarah that money."

Carolyn saved every dollar she earned from her work filling in for Dalia at the telephone office. Her wedding was coming up soon after high school graduation, and she would have to pay for all of it. Her grandparent had no extra money, and her father wouldn't lay down a single dollar for the big event. She chimed in from the stairs landing, "I'll be able to add five dollars, too."

"I have eighty in the bottom of my sock drawer." Tucker was always generous. But he rarely had any real cash to share with others.

"Tucker McBride," Betsy scolded. "I thought you stopped lying."

"I'm not lying." Tucker denied without the usual little smile that told when he was teasing. "Last summer I detasseled corn and helped pull bulbs at the gladiola farm. I worked for Butch Randolf at his Sinclair station and at Simon Winkler's Grocery. I filled in to deliver newspapers, ran errands, mowed lawns, and with my stock—."

"Ja, Tucker," Gramma patted his arm, "you did all of that. Small payments add up to large savings. Das ist *gut*."

"Let's see," Sam counted out, "your eighty, Carolyn and Betsy's five each, that leaves nine. I have four ones and a fiver in my grip." He retrieved his suitcase from the hall closet and laid it out flat on the entry hall floor. "There," he gently handed the bills to Sarah."

Sarah had listened to it all. Her eyes glistened with tears over the love her family offered. When her eyes clouded, she spoke softly. "I appreciate all of you so much. But I can't take your money. Especially not from a young boy who worked hard helping others."

Tucker shrugged like money didn't matter. "Gramma said you might get a job. When you do, you can pay me a little each week."

Sam smiled. "Banker Tucker and his two Vice Presidents, Betsy, and Carolyn will receive regular payments, I am certain."

"If I get that teaching job, I can pay you three back in a few months." She looked at Rebecca. "That is if I can stay here during that time."

"Of course, you can Sarah." Gramma raised her hand in pledge to the Lord. "At our house, there is always room for family." She laughed a little sheepishly. "That is if you don't mind sleeping in a Morris chair or in a grandson's room while he's away at boot camp."

Tucker raced up the steps, pulled open the third drawer down, fished under his white athletic socks and two pairs of argyles, and pulled out a silver-painted, wooden box with leather hinges Grandpop made a few summers back. Carolyn and Betsy retrieved from their room, their five-dollar contributions, plus Carolyn's notebook and the Reynolds ballpoint pen Birdie Kline gave her for graduation.

Tucker placed the treasure box on Gramma's cool, oval, marble-top coffee table and pulled out the stock certificate. Holding his breath, he silently counted out *seventy-seven, seventy-eight, seventy-nine, eighty. Whew, just like I remembered.*

The girls placed their five-dollar bills on top of Tucker's loot. Carolyn opened her notebook and began writing. "Received from Sarah Harter, ninety-nine dollars," she began. "In full payment of all rents owed to Ralph Wagoner to satisfy the lease on the apartment located at…?" She looked up.

"At the Wagoner House Apartments on South Main Street, Elkhart, Indiana," Grandpop filled in.

"Date it," Sam instructed, and we will all sign it." He looked intently at Ol' Ralphie. "Mr. Wagoner will be very happy to sign it too. I'm sure."

Wagoner glared at Sam and set his jaw.

Tucker shook his head. Mr. Wagoner seemed mad he was getting the money he demanded. "Why would you want to file a lawsuit instead of receiving what you wanted in the first place?"

Sam's expression changed to a knowing smile. "Cause a lawsuit would grant him additional money in the form of high interest on the unpaid balance. Now, Mr. Wagoner," he drew out in a mocking tone, "that's really how you make your money, isn't it?"

Wagoner opened his mouth to speak but Attorney Smyth jumped in, "Don't answer that, Ralph." He looked at all the loving faces staring back at him. "Just sign the paper, take your money, and let's get out of here."

"Thank you, Mr. Smyth," Sarah spoke softly. It was easy for Tucker to see she was blocking a flood of tears.

Carolyn finished writing, then started another page. She listed her own five dollars, Betsy's five, Sam's nine, and Tucker's balance making the total ninety-nine dollars. She added a statement of promise to repay and dated it. Everyone put their name on both papers. "Can I sign it too?" Tucker asked.

"It's a legal document," Gramma cautioned. "You're not old enough to sign it."

Mr. Smyth smiled. Slightly turning his back on Ralph Wagoner, he added, "I think this young fellow has shown he's man enough to sign the paper if he wants to."

Tucker smiled and savored the thought of someone calling him a *man*. He was suddenly aware; Sam was smiling too. "Sam," he whispered, "would you really have given Mr. Wagoner Maria Garcia's chief's blanket? It was Dakotah's blanket. You were keeping it for her."

"Maria took money for the blanket because she loved her children enough to let it go. She needed the money to buy food for them. I would trade the blanket to Wagoner to release Sarah from her lease because I care enough about Sarah to let it go. You and I talked about this before, Tucker. What is your Indian blanket?"

Tucker thought for a moment. *I risked getting into trouble with Gramma and Grandpop to help Bobby have a perfect day.* "Yes, Sam. I traded something valuable to me to protect a friend's secret he had shared with me."

"Then, Tucker," Sam patted the boy's broad shoulders, "I guess you are man enough to sign important papers… or be a true friend."

Man enough, Tucker mulled the words over in his head. He looked at Sam Treadway and smiled. Sam's eyes twinkled as he gave a thumbs up. *Man enough,* Tucker rehearsed again. He knew he could grow into that description. He'd been having a lot of practice lately.

Chapter Twenty-Seven
Birds of All Feathers, Flock Together

Thank goodness Gramma had fixed lunch before all the hubbub began with Wagoner and his lawyer. Usually, she put the food in a skillet or pan or baked it in a pot in the oven, then turned everything to warm or simmer. Uncle Jacob was always late to the dinner table. With eight people in and about the house, Gramma always needed a little keep-it-warm time.

Tucker looked under the lid of the pot on the back burner. Ground beef simmered in chopped onions, minced bell pepper, and tomato sauce, the perfect combination for Gramma's sloppy joes. It smelled wonderful. Two packages of hamburger buns lay closed on the counter. A large bowl of crisp potato chips, Uncle Jacob's favorite, sat beside it all.

"Tucker," Gramma cautioned, "keep your fingers out of the food. Ya daresn't eat any." She put her hands on her hips and stretched her back. Tucker often saw Gramma grabbing her back. Tucker knew she hurt. He just thought of it as normal aging.

"Sure." Tucker agreed but wondered more about his grandmother's aching back. He had to ask the next question. Grandpop had a small railroad pension and an even smaller grocery budget. Some weeks they were close on money. "Gramma ... is it okay if Bobby has lunch with us?"

"Bobby? Your bother, Bobby?" She nearly dropped the small sandwich plates she took out of the cabinet. "Is he here? Where is he?"

"Hi, Mrs. Moyer. Thanks for letting me stay for lunch," Bobby greeted. He was quiet as he came around from behind Tucker. He still had on the black wig Tucker had trimmed to look less century-one and more present-day Amish.

"Bobby? Praise the Lord." Gramma grabbed the boy and gave him a grandmother's hug. "Call me, Grandma. Tucker does."

"Yes, Ma'am."

"What's this about, Mother?" Uncle Jacob asked as he came up from the summer kitchen. He looked at Bobby with a squint of his eye.

"Well, now, Jacob," Gramma began, "Tucker's new friend, Norman, is Bobby McBride. I'd like you to meet Robert again. We haven't seen him in a very long time."

"Was ist das?" Grandpop spilled a little of his coffee on his shirt. "Let me see." He put the cup on the table and placed his hands on Bobby's shoulders. He turned Bobby's face, first to the right, then to the left. "My goodness, Ma. It is Bobby."

"You realize I have to call your mother, Bobby." Gramma looked at him squarely and yet sympathetically. "First, let's take that silly wig off your head." She reached up, took it off, and handed it to Tucker. "I always wondered about that thing." One more hug, and then she asked, "Why Bobby? Why did you run away? I expect the police will be out here today. You've been gone for two nights. A mother is frantic when she can't find her children." Looking at Tucker, she added, "And as for you, Mister, we'll talk about the part you played in all of this later."

Tucker hung his head and hoped there would still be lunch coming his way. "First of all, Bobby asked me to keep his secret," he explained. "It was another exercise God gave me in keeping my word. I had to honor what Bobby asked."

"Well, you can't fault a man for keeping his word. That's the very thing you would want him to do." Gramma patted Tucker's shoulder. "Now, to the other question." She turned to Bobby, "But…why?"

"Mom told me my dad died in the war, and I had no brothers or sisters. Then, Aunt Helen said Mom was all wrong. She said my dad lives here in Dunlap, and I have siblings. I wanted to meet Tucker and the girls. I was afraid you would send me back before I spent any time here and got to know everyone."

"You're probably right, Bobby," Gramma nodded in agreement as she walked over to the telephone. "Now, Tucker, you and Bobby get out some napkins and pour the milk. Bobby, I'll call your mother. I'll also call Sean. He was worried sick, too. They can all come here right after lunch." Gramma picked up the phone receiver. "Dalia, ring Roger Hatzinger over in Goshen, please."

Tucker heard Gramma's side of the conversation. The only part he cared about was, "Yes, he's okay. Right. That will be fine, Helen. We'll see you at two o'clock."

Everyone gathered in the dining room and made a single file to the kitchen door. The kitchen was a small, closed-off room with an entrance but no exit. So, Gramma organized an assembly line. She placed a small plate underneath, then plopped a portion of sloppy joe onto a bun using her ice cream scoop. Tiny sat on the floor under her feet, waiting for the spill that was bound to happen. Gramma passed the plate to Betsy behind her, who passed it off to the first person in the lunch line. Once they were all served, she brought the potato chip bowl into the dining room, with her own plate balanced on top.

Once Grandpop offered grace, and each had a turn at the chips, Tucker made an announcement. "It's been a long time since we've seen our little brother," Tucker announced and pointed. "You may not recognize him, but this is Bobby."

Betsy looked at Bobby through narrow eyes that focused on the tiny details. "Bobby? I thought you were Norm?"

"I was Norman for just a couple of days," Bobby admitted. "I'm Bobby McBride. And you're my sister. Wow, I never knew I would be able to say that."

Sam reached across the table and shook his hand. "Welcome to the family. I'm Rebecca's cousin. So is Sarah, but on the other side of the family."

"Glad to meet ya."

Tucker smiled as all the people he called family welcomed Bobby back to Dunlap. Bob wouldn't be in Indiana for long, but while he was there, he was home. Tucker wondered. He had never been far from home, and home was always there. Bobby was over two thousand miles away, but California never felt like home to him.

Later, Tucker and his little brother helped dry the last of the lunch dishes. Bobby smiled and said, "I liked working in the kitchen with your Gramma. That was fun."

"Drying dishes?" Tucker hadn't thought about drying dinner plates as a recreational activity. Then he realized Bobby wasn't talking about what he was doing; Bobby was talking about the company he was keeping while doing it. "Right, Bob. I think I know what you mean. I had fun too."

Tucker noticed Joe standing by the door, waiting to approve or to disapprove of whoever was knocking. When Tucker opened the door, the house still smelled of the magical scent of Gramma's spicy-sweet sloppy Joes. There, on the porch, stood Bobby's mother, her sister, and brother-in-law. Tucker recognized Martha. He had gone to his dad's house to play with Bobby when Martha and Sean were still married. That was a long time ago, but Tucker remembered. And he already knew Helen and Roger. They came to the church sometimes. They usually sat quietly in the back, but Tucker knew everyone who attended. You could hear Roger's deep baritone voice throughout the sanctuary when he sang the hymns. Roger might not say much, but everyone knew Roger was there. If Tucker didn't recognize someone, he asked Elmer Hughes, the head usher. Elmer talked to every person who came into the sanctuary, young and old. It had been a long time, but Tucker was pretty good about recognizing faces.

"Gramma," he called over his shoulder, "we have company. "Come in." As he closed the door, he saw Sean's car pull up to the door. When his father got out, Tucker saw him carrying a tiny baby.

"Come in, Dad," Tucker called out. When Sean walked in with the little one, Tucker's breath caught in his throat. Tucker wondered if his dad had carried him around in a blue blanket and a little crocheted hat when he was tiny.

"Tucker," Sean began as he pulled the blanket back from the little one's face, "this is your little brother, Matthew."

"Just like the disciple?" Tucker asked, amazed. He thought that was nice. Maybe it finally settled a long-standing question he had about his father's faith if he named his newest son after one of Jesus' followers.

"No, he's named after my brother, Matty." Sean sounded almost apologetic to Tucker. "Matty died when he was only five."

"Here's someone else you haven't seen since he was five." Tucker put his arm around Bobby's shoulder.

"Robert," Sean said with a nod and a relieved smile. "You certainly have grown. It's good to see you and even better to see you're okay and healthy. We all worried about you."

"Are you really my dad?" Bobby asked and looked down at the baby. "So," he said with a big smile, "I'm not the little brother in the family anymore. At least, not the youngest."

"Yes, I'm your dad," Sean said as he tried to take some of the heavy wrappings off little Matty. "And, I agree, you're not the youngest anymore. You lost your title of *the baby in the family*."

Gramma went into the front room, folded up the newspaper, and motioned for Sean to come. "Why don't you sit down in the living room with the baby. It'll be easier for you." She went over to the stairs leading to the second floor and called, "Carolyn, Betsy, there are some people here I want you to meet." She gently kicked Grandpop's feet out of the way. Working one of his crossword puzzles, he sat straight up with the book in his lap and his feet stretched out in front of him. "Martha, you can sit over on the couch. Helen and Roger, it's so good to see you again. Please, Tucker and Bobby will bring in some dining room chairs."

The girls came down the steps and looked around. Carolyn's eyes lit up. "May I hold the baby, Dad?" She reached for the bundle and took him in her arms. Looking at the others, she added, "Hi Helen, hi Roger. Today is the first time we've seen our new baby brother."

Tucker and Bobby quietly took seats on the floor. Tucker learned, adults sit on the chairs, and kids sit on the floor.

Martha kept looking at her son. "Bobby, do you know how much I worried?" She asked as a tear rolled down her cheeks.

"I can imagine. But not as much, or as long, as I wished I had a dad of my own and a family," Bobby whispered.

The assorted family members, all related but divided by distance and deception, sat in silence. Joe went over and curled up beside Tucker's feet. His soft hair tickled Tucker's ankle. Tiny jumped up on Gramma's lap as soon as she finally sat down on her small sewing rocker.

Tucker tried to put the different people together. Gramma, Grandpop, Uncle Jacob, Sarah, and Sam were related to Tucker, Betsy, Tim, and Carolyn. Sam and Sarah were not kin of each other. Martha was the only kin of

Bobby, Helen, and Roger. No one in Tucker's house was related to Martha, Helen, and Roger, except Bobby. Sean was, or once was, a relative of everyone. They were either his children, his ex-wife, his ex-sister and brother-in-law, or ex-mother and father-in-law. That made even Sarah and Sam distant cousins from long ago. Tucker wondered if everyone could keep all this motley group of people straight.

Chapter Twenty-Eight
We Don't Know, What We Don't Know

Later, when the house was quiet, and the girls and Grandpop had gone up to bed, Tucker helped Gramma put coffee cups into the kitchen sink. "Gramma?"

"Ja, Tucker?" Gramma stopped. Her hand still rested on the handle of the pitcher pump. "Is something wrong? I think you did a very unselfish thing today, offering Sarah your money."

Tucker felt awful and didn't look at his grandmother in the face. "Thanks, but…I lied to you a lot the last two days, and I'm sorry."

"Oh, you lied to me?"

"Well…yes, about Bobby."

"Did I ask you if you had been with Bobby today or yesterday?"

"No. But you said Dad and Bobby's mom were worried because he was missing." His voice fell off at the end. "I didn't say he was right here eating your food and sitting at your table."

"Why didn't you, Tucker? You didn't tell a lie. You didn't tell us anything."

"Bobby said he wanted to spend some time with me. He said, if his mom found out where he was, his mother would make him come home."

"Ja," Gramma agreed. "She would want him to be safe."

"Gramma, he'd be safe here, with us." Tucker followed her into the living room. "Bobby's mom told him

Dad died in the war, and he had no brothers or sisters. He just wanted to have a big family for a few hours. I promised him I wouldn't tell."

"That's the predicament* we get ourselves in. You promised something to someone and didn't realize it could get complicated." His grandmother put her hand on Tucker's shoulder. "There are no easy answers in life, Tucker. Truth isn't a relative term, depending on what we believe or want. Truth is truth."

"I guess I know what you mean, Gramma. There's my truth, and then there's Vinny Wagoner's truth."

"Ja, that's right. Sometimes the truth can harm people, so we have to decide what we should tell. Gossips may tell truths, but that doesn't make it right to hurt others. In the war, a captured soldier couldn't tell the truth about where his fellow soldiers were. So, the enemy would punish him for staying quiet. With kids and their parents, silence is usually not an option either. I don't want you to lie to me, but I'm proud that you kept your word to Bobby."

"Thanks, Gramma."

Gramma spoke softly. "Even Jesus knew it would be hard not to lie. He told Peter he knew Peter would deny even knowing him, not once, but three times. Jesus even knew when it would happen, before morning, when the rooster would announce the new day." *

"I remember that." Tucker felt some relief. Maybe Peter felt like Tucker did. He smiled when he thought of the Bible stories Mrs. Kline taught in her Sunday school class.

"One night, the chief priests and elders sent a mob carrying swords and handmade clubs." He added, "I bet Jesus' friends were scared."

Tucker sat down on the footstool and shook his head. "Peter and some of the other disciples were supposed to stand guard while Jesus prayed. But his friends fell asleep, so they didn't see the crowd and the Sanhedrin guards coming."

Gramma slowly sank onto the corner of the couch. "What did Peter do when the guards took Jesus away?"

"He followed," Tucker answered. "That's when a couple of servant girls asked Peter if he wasn't one of Jesus' followers. Peter said, 'No, I don't even know him.'"

Tucker put his hand up. "When those around Peter asked again about Jesus, Peter got mad and used some words he probably shouldn't have. They asked, 'Hey, you're one of his friends, aren't you?' Peter said, 'Not me. I don't know the man.'"

Tucker whispered, "Then Peter heard a rooster crow and remembered what Jesus said. Jesus already told Peter that he would deny him three times before the rooster crowed. Peter went out and cried."

Gramma sat in her rocker and smoothed her hand over the worn leather of her Bible. "Why do you think Peter denied he was a friend of the Lord? You know he lied."

"I guess he was afraid they'd take him off to jail, too. So, Peter protected himself."

"That's probably a good reason. But we don't know the reasons why Peter lied. Life isn't that simple. It's enough to know, Jesus knew Peter would not always tell the truth. Still, Jesus made Peter one of the leaders of the early church."

Tucker was surprised with a new understanding. "Wow, I guess Jesus knew Peter better than we do."

"Jesus knew Peter better than Peter knew himself," Gramma said with a laugh. "Tucker, to be loyal to a friend who asks you to keep a secret, you can end up caught in the middle of something you don't understand. Sometimes, we must finally tell the truth. We don't know the whole story behind a secret."

"I found that out." Deep inside, Tucker knew that Gramma didn't understand why he had agreed to keep Bobby's secret. That was okay. God knew why. Most of the time, Gramma and Grandpop were enough for him. But Tucker wanted to complete his entire family.

Tucker had tried to put his family together for the last few years. First, Joe, his war dog, finally came home after the big World War ended. Earlier that day, all the members of his family group sat there in his living room, all thanks to a man who had never been a father to Tucker since he was five months old. Maybe *family* was far more than Tucker could ever have imagined. Grandpop always said, "We are too soon old and too late smart."

Maybe Tucker got a little older and a little wiser that day. Maybe, somehow, we're all *family*, all trying to understand each other. We want to love each other, regardless of how we're related. Or, maybe we don't even have to understand. For the first time, he knew what Pastor Dailey meant by *the family of God*. Perhaps we need to spend some time with *family* of all connections, on some very perfect day.

Chapter Twenty-Nine
The Trees Were Full of Flocks of Every Kind

Early that Sunday morning, Tucker rolled over and looked at the ceiling. The white paint was not as bright as it once was. Gramma and Grandpop didn't have the extra money to touch up chipped paint or scratched doors when Tiny wanted outside. That was okay. Joe found a way to get his nose around the screen door of the summer kitchen and open it to the backyard. Joe was the usual family member who let the littlest dog out.

Most of all, it was home for all those who lived there. And *home* was a special word to Tucker. It described more than the large white house on the corner with a wide porch like a friendly smile. *Home* was belonging, regardless of who else lived there.

Sunday morning meant one thing to Tucker and his family, church. Just a few steps across the side street from the house, it was Tucker's second home. It was a busy place, with Sunday morning worship and Sunday school, Ladies Aide Society meetings, quilting bees during the winter before the quilts got too hot to hold on their laps, and Christmas Bazaars. Tucker helped Grandpop perform many janitorial tasks. Tending to the furnace was a major winter responsibility for his grandfather. In the spring Tucker would help his ninety-year-old grandfather clean old ashes out of the furnace. Or, Grandpop was on the roof, repairing shingles and pulling tennis balls out of the gutters. Tucker was usually at his grandfather's side, whether up or down, inside, or out. Tucker lived at the church as much as he did at home.

It was Sunday morning as Tucker jumped out of bed and chose a nice tan pull-over sweater to go with his brown slacks. Aunt Cora, Uncle Jerry, and his cousin Luke always came for Sunday dinner after church. After the service, Aunt Cora would hurry home to take the hot vegetable out of the oven she had waiting for lunch. Tucker would change into Levi's and a T-shirt after they ate, so he and Luke could play baseball in the sandlot near the house. Usually, Betsy joined them with her baseball glove if she didn't have to babysit.

Tucker knew Betsy was growing up and seemed to like girlie things. But he also knew the Fort Wayne Women's Baseball team, the Daisies, offered her a tryout. Gramma said, "No," but Betsy knew the invitation was an honor. Since her joining the team would mean a lot of travel, leaving Indiana, and being away from home, Betsy knew she wasn't ready for that.

Joe waited at Tucker's door, patient but wagging his tail. "Let's find breakfast, boy," Tucker announced as he opened the door and bounded down the steps.

When he got to the kitchen, Tucker got a medium-sized mixing bowl out of the cabinet and reached for the Wheaties box. He could have found the cereal with his eyes closed since the Breakfast of Champions was his every morning meal and anytime snack.

"Tucker," Sarah came into the room and hugged Tucker's arm. "Thank you, thank you, thank you, again. If you hadn't spoken up yesterday, Smyth would file a lawsuit against me tomorrow."

"That's okay," Tucker said as his face grew hot and a little pinker than usual. "It just didn't make any sense to me."

"It didn't make sense to any of us, Tucker," Sam joined in. "But you're the only one who came up with a solution. You didn't just sit in the boat and try to fish with no bate."

"Tucker likes people and helps them when he can." Grandpop reached for a piece of toast Gramma had already buttered. "I'd better get over to the church. With all the hubbub yesterday, I didn't get to run a dust mop down the hall."

"I'll help you, Grandpop." Tucker offered, wiped his mouth, washed the bowl in the sink, and put it back in the cabinet.

"Wait a minute, Tucker," Sam called to him. "I have something for you."

"I'll be over in a minute." He helped his grandfather put his coat on over his dark blue suit. That was Grandpop's usual cold weather church attire. There was one other suit hanging in his grandfather's closet, in charcoal black, but that was all. There was no need for a railroad foreman to dress in fancy clothes to go out and rebuild damaged bridges in Ohio, Indiana, and Illinois. Summer church clothing was a little different. It consisted of a short-sleeve button-up shirt with a button-down collar, and summer-weight slacks.

"Here, Tucker," Sam offered as he gave him something all wrapped up in brown paper.

"What is it?" Tucker looked from the package to Sam. "Why?"

"It's a jacket Harvey Turnbull made for me out of a deer hide. I was given the hide by a hunter I know out in Colorado." He smiled and helped pull the paper off the jacket. "I noticed how small your coat was getting. You need this deerskin coat more than I do."

Tucker couldn't believe his eyes. It was the jacket he dreamed about like John Wayne wore in many of his western movies. The tan, buckskin suede coat, detailed with deerskin fringe, amazed Tucker more than he could imagine. Slipping his arms into the sleeves, Tucker inhaled the rich, earthy, slightly sweet aroma of the leather. Immediately he imagined himself on the back of a palomino, riding through the Texas hill country, west of Austin and north of San Antonio. The hot, southwestern breeze blew through the trees, his hair, and set the fringe on the jacket dancing. A broad smile covered his entire face. "It is amazing. Thank you."

"Oh Sam, no. It is much too expensive." Gramma lightly touched Tucker's arm.

"No, Becca. The hide cost me nothing, and the sewing was free too," Sam explained. "Tucker acted like a man when he kept his word. He's growing and needs a coat that fits, a man's coat he can grow into."

A man's coat. That sounded good to Tucker.

"Well," his grandmother drew out slowly, "I guess it will be okay." She hugged Tucker. "He is growing into a man."

Tucker liked the way it fit, too big but comfortably roomy. He had room to wear it next year, too, before he outgrew it. He buttoned the coat and started to go out the door. Stopping, he turned. "Thanks again, Sam."

"You earned it, Tucker." Sam closed the door behind him.

Across the street and up the steps, Tucker breezed in through the door. "Grandpop?"

His grandfather came into the hall from the sanctuary. "Looks *gut* in there," he said. "I guess we did a *gut* job before we left last Sunday. No one was in the church on Beggars' Night. The apple bobbing activity and bleachers were all set up in the parking lot."

"Well, now Grandpop, here's the thing."

"What thing is that, Tucker?" His grandfather checked the waste paper basket in the hall. "You mean, the thing about when you and your friends were down in the church basement last evening?"

"Yep, that's the thing," Tucker admitted sheepishly. "How did you know? I didn't see anyone in the church."

"I could see the light in the furnace room from the house and came over to check on it." Grandpop continued to check all corners of the hallway for pieces of debris. A small piece of paper near the baseboard found its way into the basket. "What were you doing? It's cold down there. I didn't even fire up the heat until yesterday. The mornings especially are cool. Mrs. Frederick's mother would soon let me know. As people get older, they seem to be cold all the time."

Maybe it's just Mrs. Frederick's mother, Tucker thought but kept it to himself. "We went on through the basement, past the furnace." Tucker dusted off a table with his handkerchief as he passed. Elmer Hughes had placed a display of fliers and brochures in fan shapes on the table. "I was curious about what was back in the corner of the space down in the basement."

"Curiosity will get your hand caught in the mousetrap someday, Tucker." He stood back and inspected the front hall again. "I thought you were in every corner of this building by now."

"Not the back room."

"Anything interesting?"

"Well, yes. There was a wooden grave marker… Elizabeth Naomi Yoder, Born 1792. Died 1837. I thought that was interesting."

"A tombstone?" Grandpop stopped and searched the ceiling for a memory hiding there. "I haven't been in that corner of the basement for a long time, either."

"Well, not a stone." Tucker corrected him. "It was made of wood."

"Hum… Yoder. I don't think—"

"I already found the family. When we were out at the corn maze, Frank Moody said Elizabeth Yoder was his very distant grandmother."

His grandfather smiled and shook his head. "Tucker, you know every detail I taught you, plus all the stories people have told you. You could write a history book about the people in Dunlap."

"Morning, Joseph." Pastor Dailey breezed in the door with Sunday morning energy and shook Joseph's hand. "Tucker, morning to you, too."

"Hi, Pastor Dailey. Do you need anything this morning?"

"Thanks, Tucker. No. Can't think of a thing. God is in His Heaven, and all's right with the world."

Freddie came in, followed by Christy. "Are we going to sit down here this Sunday or up in the balcony?" Christy asked. "We are apple bobbing winners. Maybe we should sit with the grown-ups. Where to?" she asked as she hung her coat on the coat rack. "Wow, where did you get such a great jacket, Tucker?"

Tucker smoothed his hand over the coarse grain of the suede, unbuttoned it, but did not take it off. "Sam gave it to me a little while ago."

"Fantastic." She checked the coat all around. "It looks absolutely super."

Aunts, uncles, cousins, neighbors, and friends all began to gather for worship. It had been a good and safe weekend. Tucker raised his eyebrows when Sarah and Sam came in together. Not because they walked into the sanctuary at the same time. But because they came in holding hands. *Wow*, he breathed out slowly. *That's what all the looks and giggles were about.*

Gramma came in carrying a stack of music. She hurried past those still standing in the hall and made her way to the organ in the sanctuary. The new instrument was still a puzzle. It was much more complicated than the old pump organ she used to play. The previous organ required sitting at the keyboard and pumping the pedals near the floor with her feet. The new organ had drawbars she had to pull out and two keyboards. She modified her music to make it as simple as possible. She was soon going to retire and let James's daughter take over the accompaniment for worship. In the meantime, she had to prove to herself that she could play the Hammond organ.

"Can I carry the music for you, Gramma?" Tucker asked as he quickly followed his grandmother a few steps.

"I think I'm okay. If I pass it to you, I'll probably drop it."

"Well? Where are we going to sit?" Christy asked again.

"I think I'd like to sit down here, with Grandpop. Why don't you guys sit with Grandpop and me?"

"Super. I don't think I want to sit by Anna anyway. She's probably still complaining about not winning the apple bobbing contest." Christy looked at Freddie. "Sorry, Freddie."

"That's all right." He looked up just as some new people came in. The Riley family entered with Kathy Marie Riley in the lead.

"Hi Freddie," Kathy said as she caught up to the three.

Freddie's freckles turned red. "Hi, Kathy Marie. You want to sit with us?"

"Sure." Kathy looked back at her mother. "We're all going to sit together."

"Good. We'll all take up several pews." Her mother held Braxton's hand more tightly. "You're staying with us, Braxton."

Kathy explained, "Dad wanted to thank you all so much for helping us yesterday. We decided to come to worship in your church. He said, 'Where good people are grown.' He decided the pastor must teach good living here."

Tucker heard a familiar voice come up behind him. "Good morning."

"Bobby," Tucker turned and grabbed his brother in a wrestling hug. "How? You didn't run away again, did you?"

"Nope." Bob turned and pointed toward the door. "Mom, Aunt Helen, and Uncle Roger ...we all came."

"Hi, Bobby." Christy rocked up and down, heel and toe, excited.

They gathered in close, hugging and slapping each other joyfully on the back. As the hour grew close to the introit*, they all moved toward the front of the sanctuary. Grandpop had already taken his seat near the pulpit on the left. Tucker came around from the other end of the pew and slid into the seat beside him, followed by Christy, Bobby, and Freddie. Martha, Helen, and Roger sat behind them.

Gramma started playing the processional. The energizing music filled the room.

Tucker closed his eyes. The morning was peaceful. Bitty Miller's two large arrangements of lavender and white fall chrysanthemums graced the alter. Their earthy, herby aroma drifted to where Tucker and his friends sat. For the first time, he felt whole. Bobby was able to come without running away. They were all together.

Pastor Dailey raised his hands. "Please stand."

The choir entered from the back of the sanctuary and processed up the center aisle. Everyone sang, "Holy, Holy, Holy! Lord God Almighty."

Halfway through the hymn, Grandpop stepped out of the way to let another person join them in the pew. Tucker looked up from his hymnal and nearly dropped it. As they all sang verse three, Vinny Wagoner squeezed in between him and his grandfather. Tucker saw his grandfather offer to share his hymnal with Vinny.

When Vinny started singing, Tucker's voice choked up. Vinny sounded great. Tucker thought his voice sounded like Eddy Arnold, a favorite of Tucker's from the Grand Ol' Opry.

Rev. Daily stepped back into the pulpit. "Please read Psalm 118:24 with me." Each member of the congregation joined him as they read together from their bulletin. "This is the day the Lord has made. Let us rejoice and be glad in it.' You may be seated."

"Vinny," Tucker whispered. "You can really sing."

Vinny mouthed, "Thanks." Vinny's head was down, embarrassed. He whispered, "And thanks for not telling on me to my dad. Dad said he was at your house yesterday. You and your grandmother promised not to tell if I came to church. You both kept your word."

Grandpop gave Tucker that *special church look*. The boys stopped whispering.

To Tucker, the whole room seemed full, full of family and full of friends, all wrapped up in a chief's blanket to show he was loyal to his friends. Pastor Daily opened the Bible and read Psalm 118:24 again. *This is the day that the Lord has made.* Tucker listened and thought, *I had a perfect day because I lived His day fully. The Lord made it. If I fill every day with living, helping others, loving, and forgiving, I will recognize every one of His perfect days and claim them for my own.*

Epilogue

***The house on the corner sat safely back from the road.
It was one of those big white square homes that spoke
the language of family and love and welcomed everyone.***

Tucker McBride is a fictional character modeled after my husband, Bill Rapp, who grew up in Dunlap, Indiana. Dunlap is a small community between Elkhart and Goshen, Indiana. He and his brother Jack, and sisters, Merry and Beverly, reared by their grandparents after their mother died, saw their dad, Edgar, occasionally, although he lived a few miles away. Bill was seven months old when his mother, Helen, died. She was twenty-seven.

Most of the events in *Tucker's Perfect Day* happened but at different times. I condensed some of the events and took some of them out of chronological order to fit the story. Since I wasn't there, I don't know the actual dialogue. These stories are consistent with the character and behavior of Albert and Perninnah Kime. Their background is Pennsylvania Dutch, therefore the Dutch or German words, unusual phrases, and pronunciations.

Bill's half-brother Edger Rapp, Jr (called Joe by the family) moved back from California at about twenty-five. He grew up believing his father died in WWII, and he had no siblings. Joe met their father once again before their dad died at age fifty-nine. I included Joe in this story to represent his move back home, to be near family.

Bill, like Tucker, did learn that family, neighbors, friends, and church family all go together to make up the Family of God. Enjoy them all, regardless of who makes up your family.

"This is the day that the Lord hath made. I will rejoice and be glad in it." Psalm 118:24 KJV

Doris Jean Gaines Rapp

Glossary and References

Babes-in-a-Blanket – handkerchief folding. I made these as a child too.

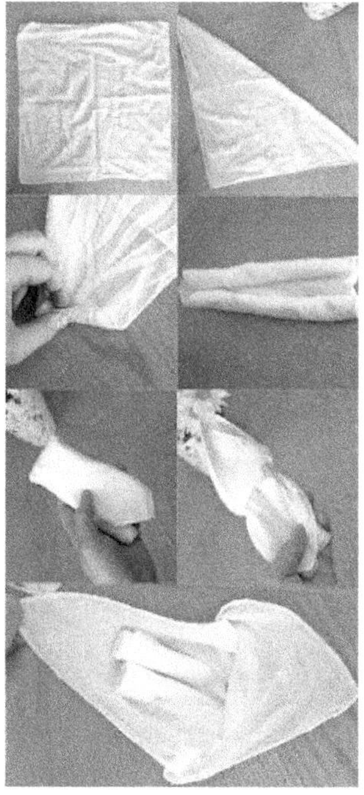

Bank barn – a barn built into a hill or other sloped ground

 brown striped, tan stoneware bowl

Chip-tin – A large round metal can, sold with potato chips in it
Clark, Walter van Tilburg. (1940) The Ox-Box Incident (movie)

Clodhoppers – large, heavy lace-up shoes

<u>das</u> <u>ist</u> <u>gut</u> (Pennsylvania Dutch) - meaning that/this is good)

dummkopf (Pennsylvania Dutch and German) - meaning dumb idiot)

Reginald Heber 1826 (Words) and John B. Dykes 1861 (Music). "Holy, Holy, Holy! Lord God Almighty."

Epitaph – Words written on a tombstone that describe the individual or their favorite words.

Ford Woody – Several car makers made station wagons in the 1930s and 1940s with wood paneling on both sides. There was none more popular than the Ford Mercury Woody.

Frigidaire – A refrigerator made by the GM Company, still made today.

Hue – color

Introit – The first song of a church service. The choir often marches in on while singing it.

Medusa – In Greek mythology, Medusa (Gorgo) was one of three monstrous Gorgons. Her hair was snakes.

In 1891, Edward Canby and Orange O. Ozias, two businessmen from Dayton, Ohio, purchased the patents for the newly invented computing scale and incorporated the Computing Scale Company to manufacture commercial scales. Later, the company became part of IBM. Orange O.

Ozias' initials were O. O. O. Perfect initials for someone who owns a scale company. Jim Savage posted on Facebook: Dayton Ohio 50's - 60's – 70's - and 80's. 5/10/21

Model A (Ford) with rumble seat:

The author took these pictures in a Walmart parking lot on 5/19/2021

Moreish – creating a desire to want more of something

Pilfered (pilfer) – to steal things of little value

Piper Cub Cockpit   The controls of a small airplane

Predicament – An embarrassing, hard, or unpleasant situation

Rooster: A male bird of the chicken family. When the rooster crows three times. – Matthew 26:58-75

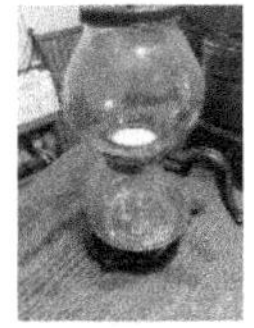

Silex - vacuum coffee maker

Song by N. Simon/C. Tobias - The Old Lamplighter- 1946

Treadle sewing machine -

[1] The North Wind Doth Blow - By Anonymous British Author – some attribute to Mother Goose

Ya daresn't loss it. – Pennsylvania Dutch - You dare not lose it.

Was ist das? - *What is this* in German. The "w" sounds like "v."

Recipes

Beans and Ham
Soak a pound of great northern white beans overnight
Cover beans with water and bring to a boil. Cover with pan lid, turn to simmer
(Or, use presoaked Randall Great Northern beans purchased in a jar
Add tablespoon chopped sweet onion
Cube a half-pound to a pound of lean ham (amount depends on your taste)
Cook, covered for an hour or until beans are tender

Sweet Cornbread
Melt 1 stick (= ½ cup) of butter in a cast-iron skillet
In a bowl mix:
1 cup all-purpose flour
1 cup yellow cornmeal
2/3 cup sugar
1 teaspoon salt
3 ½ teaspoons baking powder
1 egg
1 cup milk
Mix all together
Add half the melted butter (4 T) - mix
Pour all into the cast-iron skillet with the butter at the bottom.
Bake in 400 degrees, preheated oven for 20-25 minutes or until a toothpick inserted into the center comes out clean.

Hamburger Stroganoff

Ingredients:
1-pound lean ground beef
1 small onion chopped or half a medium
1 teaspoon salt
¼ teaspoon pepper
2 – 3 tablespoon flour
2 cans cream of mushroom soup
Milk – fill the 2 soup cans about ¾ full
1 cup sour cream
1 package noodle or homemade noodles

Mix:
Brown and break apart hamburger in a large skillet
Added chopped onion while browning
Add salt and pepper
After the meat has browned, add 2 – 3 tablespoons flour to absorb all the liquid – mix well
Add the 2 cans of mushroom soup
Add milk and mix all together well
Turn to simmer (make sure not boiling) and simmer for 15-20 min.
Add sour cream
Cook noodles to desired tenderness
Put a serving of noodles on a plate, then ladle several large cooking spoonsful of stroganoff
Serve with a vegetable for a complete meal

Pineapple Bread

¾ cup whole milk warmed to about 110°F
2¼ teaspoon active dry yeast or instant yeast (1 standard packet)
1 cup granulated sugar
½ cup packed light or dark brown sugar
5 tablespoons unsalted butter, softened to room temperature, and cut into 5 pieces
½ teaspoon pure vanilla extract
2 large eggs, at room temperature
1 teaspoon salt
1¼ teaspoon ground cinnamon
½ teaspoon ground nutmeg
½ teaspoon ground allspice
3½ cups all-purpose flour or bread flour (spoon & leveled)
1 cup dry pineapple – cut into small pieces.
ICING
1 cup confectioners' sugar
3 tablespoons fresh or bottled pineapple juice (or use milk and a splash of vanilla extract for plain icing). For thick icing reduce the juice to 1T.

1. Dough. Whisk milk, yeast, and 1t granulated sugar in a mixer bowl fitted with a dough hook
2. Add – brown sugar, butter, vanilla, eggs, salt, cinnamon, nutmeg, allspice, and 1 cup flour. Beat on low for 30 seconds scraping sides of the bowl as you go. Add the remaining flour and the pineapple. Beat on medium speed until the dough comes together and pulls away from the sides of the bowl, - about 2 minutes. The dough should be a little sticky and soft. If too sticky so not pulling away, mix in a little flour 1 tablespoon at a time.

3. Knead dough. Keep in the bowl and beat another 2 minutes or knead by hand on a lightly floured surface for 2 min.
4. Let rise. Lightly grease a large bowl with oil or nonstick spray. Place dough in the bowl, turning it to coat all sides in the oil. Cover bowl with aluminum foil, plastic wrap, or a clean kitchen towel. Let dough rise in a relatively warm environment for 1-2 hours or until double in size.
5. Grease a 9x13 baking pan or two 9-inch square or round baking pans.
6. Shape the rolls. When ready, punch down the dough to release the air. Divide the dough into 14-16 equal parts. Shape each piece into t smooth ball, pinching it on the bottom to seal. Arrange in the baking pan.
7. Rise again. Cover rolls with aluminum foil, plastic wrap, or a clean kitchen towel. Allow rolls to rise until puffy – about 1 hour.
8. Preheat oven to 350°F
9. Bake the rolls. For 20-25 minutes or until golden brown on top. Rotating pan halfway through.
10. Make the icing. Whisk the icing ingredients together, then drizzle or brush on warm rolls. If you want thicker icing, reduce the juice to 1tablespoon. Serve immediately.
11. Cover the leftover rolls tightly and store them at room temperature for 1-2 days or in the refrigerator for up to 1 week.

Popcorn Balls

1 cup sugar
½ cup white corn syrup
1/3 cup water
¼ cup butter
¾ teaspoon salt
¾ teaspoon vanilla
3 quarts of unseasoned popcorn
Combine and stir until sugar is dissolved – continue cooking without stirring until forms a brittle ball (270) I used (260). Add vanilla and stir only enough to mix.
Drizzle the cooked syrup over popcorn. Mix well. Wet the hands slightly. Press into balls.

Rike's Chocolate Cake

This recipe was in The Middletown Journal at least 40 years ago. Said to be the same as Rike's Chocolate Cake

Ingredients:
1/2 cup butter
3 eggs
2 1/2 cup sugar
5 1/2 squares Hershey baking chocolate
2 1/2 cup cake flour
2 teaspoon baking powder
1 1/2 cup sweet milk (whole milk as distinguished from butter- or sour- milk)
1 teaspoon salt
1 cup nut meats – walnuts or pecans
2 teaspoon vanilla

1.   Cream butter and sugar, add the egg yolk, and

> beat well
2.   Add melted chocolate and beat
3.   Add flour and milk alternately
4.   Beat egg whites
5.   Add vanilla and nuts
6.   Fold in beaten egg whites
7.   Add baking powder – alone and last
8.   Mix using an electric beater at medium speed

Preheat oven to 375 degrees
Bake for 45 minutes in a 9 x13 greased and floured pan
-or for 25 minutes in 2 9-inch greased and floured layer
pans

Chocolate Icing
6 tablespoon brown sugar
3 tablespoon cocoa
3 tablespoon butter
3 tablespoon cream
powdered sugar
Melt brown sugar, cocoa, butter, and cream together
Add enough powdered sugar to give the mixture the
consistency of frosting

Rike's Sloppy Joes
2# gr beef
1/2 # onions chopped
1/8 # bell pepper - diced
1 1/2 cup Catsup
1 teaspoon salt
1/4 cup sugar
1/8 cup vinegar
1/4 cup dry mustard
Brown meat, add bell pepper and onions.
Add catsup, salt, sugar, vinegar, and dry mustard. Mix and
simmer until thickened - about an hour/ Approx. - 12
servings

Enjoy. Sometimes I like to substitute a little Sweet Baby Rays for some of the catsup. A little snappier.

Amish Friendship Bread
This sweet, cinnamon bread requires waiting ten days as you knead and feed a starter.
I found a no-starter recipe on the Internet: (https://www.friendshipbreadkitchen.com/no-starter-starter-free-amish-friendship-bread/ - accessed 5/29/2021). I include it here.
Makes two loaves. Preheat oven to 325° (165° C)
Ingredients:
3 large eggs
1 cup oil
1½ cups buttermilk (Or add 1½ tablespoons of lemon juice to 1½ cups of milk)
1 cup sugar
½ teaspoon vanilla
2 teaspoons cinnamon
1½ teaspoon baking powder
½ teaspoon salt
½ teaspoon baking soda
2 cups flour
1 small box instant vanilla pudding (can use 2 boxes to boost flavor and moisture)
1 cup nuts chopped (optional – pecans or walnuts)
1 cup raisins (optional)
 Instructions
1. Preheat oven to 325° (165° C)
2. In a large mixing bowl, add ingredients
3. Grease two large loaf pans
4. Dust the greased pans with an additional mixture of ½ cup sugar and ½ teaspoon cinnamon
5. Pour batter evenly into two loaf pans or cake pans and sprinkle the remaining cinnamon-sugar mixture on top.

6. Bake – 1 hour or until bread loosens evenly from sides and a toothpick inserted in center comes out clean
7. Cool 15 minutes before turning over onto a cooling rack. Upright immediately
8. Delicious – Enjoy!